Anonymous

My Love, she's but a Lassie

Vol. 1

Anatiposi

Anonymous

My Love, she's but a Lassie

Vol. 1

Reprint of the original, first published in 1875.

1st Edition 2024 | ISBN: 978-3-38283-094-6

Anatiposi Verlag is an imprint of Outlook Verlagsgesellschaft mbH.

Verlag (Publisher): Outlook Verlag GmbH, Zeilweg 44, 60439 Frankfurt, Deutschland
Vertretungsberechtigt (Authorized to represent): E. Roepke, Zeilweg 44, 60439 Frankfurt, Deutschland
Druck (Print): Books on Demand GmbH, In de Tarpen 42, 22848 Norderstedt, Deutschland

MY LOVE, SHE'S BUT A LASSIE.

BY

THE AUTHOR OF

"QUEENIE."

"Like to the grass that's newly sprung,
Or like a tale that's new begun,
Or like the bird that's here to-day,
Or like the pearlèd dew of May:
. . . . .
E'en such is man; who lives by breath,
Is here, now there, in life, and death—
The grass withers, the tale is ended;
The bird is flown, the dew's ascended."
SIMON WASTELL.

IN THREE VOLUMES.

VOL. I.

LONDON:
HURST AND BLACKETT, PUBLISHERS,
13, GREAT MARLBOROUGH STREET.
1875.

LONDON :
PRINTED BY MACDONALD AND TUGWELL,
BLENHEIM HOUSE.

MY LOVE, SHE'S BUT A LASSIE.

CHAPTER I.

"My friend, I have seen a white crane bigger!
She was the smallest lady alive,
Made in a piece of nature's madness,
Too small, almost, for the life and gladness
That over-filled her."

R. BROWNING.

ONE August afternoon, precisely at the time when the 4.15 train was bound to leave the busy, over-crowded Middleland Junction, Walter Huntley, Captain in one of Her Majesty's cavalry regiments, quietly stepped into an empty carriage. Having already seen a portmanteau and tin case—both of which bore marks of many a

journey in dints, weather-stains, and labels
with strange foreign names—put into the
van, he established himself in the shadiest
corner, on that hot afternoon, prepared to
enjoy all the comic papers, and one of the
most amusing pamphlets of a living Ameri-
can humourist.

The time was up!—so the train, being
"rather" a punctual one, might not probably start for five or six minutes yet; but
no one had ever known Wat Huntley to
be either fussily early or languidly late,
being, as he was, a happy example of
pleasant, easy punctuality. He had some
other good qualities too—strong and lasting
ones,—but as these were not of the kind
which show on the surface, or mark out
their owner among the world-crowd of
men, passers-by were likely enough to ap-
praise him mentally at one glance—and not
look again. They had only seen an indifferent figure, and a face which friends termed
"not good-looking," acquaintance called

"plain," but ill-natured people and enemies downrightly said was " ugly !"—For, of course, he had some enemies, as what obstinately honest man may not have ?—albeit one of the best-bred, most upright, and most simply God-fearing gentlemen to be met with easily in the British Isles.

Just now he watched the belated passengers; chuckling to himself at their hurry with almost boyish amusement, being a simple-hearted soul.

"That white-haired old gentleman seems utterly bewildered. Why don't the ladies look after him?—poor old man! How their maid *is* rating the porter! (I suppose their ball-finery is ruined.) That's his daughter, most likely—tall, languid, washed-out. A little girl too—younger sister, perhaps —but, by Jove! *what* hair she has !" For, as he looked out, a stray gleam of sunlight, coming through the glass roof, lit up such wondrous reddened, yellowish tresses, in which prisoned sunbeams seemed playing

MY LOVE, SHE'S BUT A LASSIE.

VOL. I.

pitchfork; and it would puzzle anyone to say whether she was ugly or a beauty. Perfect creamy complexion (like some picture of a girl in a window, by old Titian); but I fancy a shy, defiant little puss. Ugly has it, I believe. But what a shame of her aunt, or whoever she is, to keep her there!"

And Wat Huntley, who especially hated to see children or animals tyrannised over, glanced with strong disapprobation at the elder lady, who,—herself seated in shade,— looked, with her long oval face, smooth hair of a light nearly hueless tint, and a cool, dust-coloured travelling dress, the very essence of refined repose and selfish, lady-like calmness.

At last he bent forward, and asked her leave to give his place to the young lady.

The faded Madonna whom he addressed raised her downcast lids, and looked at him with a sort of serious sweetness; then thanked him in her foreign accent, but said it was sufficient the girl should take another seat;

which, obeying a slight gesture, her somewhat wild-looking, rustic little companion
accordingly did, with a manner between a
school-girl's brusqueness and the movement
of an automaton.

"Tyrannised over!" thought Wat to himself; again settling back to the enjoyment of
his comic paper. "I never like these women
with faces like sign-boards of saintliness;
besides, her eyes are so small and set close
together, and her mouth the same, and thin-
lipped. Nothing honest or genial about
her kind." From which it may be perceived that Huntley was given to a closer in-
spection of strangers than most people; nay
more, he was generally so convinced of the
correctness of his own first impressions that,
once really formed, he was seldom known to
change them.

All at once, to his secret dismay, he found
himself addressed; and perceived that the
slight remark he had only made to quiet a
troublesome conscience, was to be, in the

lady's eyes, merely the prelude to an interesting conversation, on such topics as
the weather or the country around; the few
which we islanders wisely hold to be not
productive of over-intimacy with our fellow-
travellers, who ought generally, when un-
known, to be distrusted.

To his dismay!—because, although too
much a gentleman not to be quite at his
ease in the society of any lady, it was yet
an undoubted fact that he greatly preferred
a mess-room, or even solitude in his own
quarters, and "being left to himself." The
verdict of his brother officers, when closely
questioned by fair cross-examiners as to the
reason of his absence from most of the
petty gatherings for flirtation and gossip,
offered in many country quarters, was always
the same; viz., that "Captain Huntley was
a very good fellow indeed; but that he did
not care for ladies' society." One or two,
however, may have held very private
opinions as to the cause which produced

this effect; for these being specially gifted with good looks and well-built figures—advantages which were supposed to counter-balance all other considerations in the female mind, excepting those of fortune and title!—had persuaded themselves, with secret self-satisfaction, that—since Wat was known to honestly hate being beaten in most things in which he did take part—it was presumably a sense of physical inferiority which prevented him from entering lists where they *must* be winners !

Despite these prevailing notions, it was in truth more from chance at first, and then from habit, that our friend had grown to be thought a misogynist; and no one had a truer veneration for his own female relatives, or a stronger belief in their perfections. For him, they were women apart from the rest of the world—as the memory of an innocent childhood in the green time long, long ago, is apart from the eager, toiling, disappointed, worn-out life of manhood.

He liked other things better than society, which was always changing; that was all. His work, for instance (for he did all things thoroughly), and some studies at times; and his regiment, which was indisputably the finest, and with the best set of brother-officers, in the service. His parts might not be brilliant in matters requiring powerful intellect, brought to bear on specially abstruse subjects; nor had he strength corresponding to the stature of an Anakim. But, though he had secret higher ambitions, he did know at present that he was a thorough soldier; was as straight a shot as most, and perhaps a better player at billiards; while as to riding—honest Wat Huntley was not given to vanity, but he secretly owned to himself, with a well-pleased boyish smile, though he was within a little of thirty, that "if there was one thing he did fancy he could do—if there was—he should say he knew how to ride."

No wonder, therefore, that while this

strange, and also not especially attractive lady plied him with apparently general questions, to which he was bound to answer, Wat wished most heartily that she— wouldn't.

What a lawyer, to conduct a snaky, cunning cross-examination and extract information from monosyllábic witnesses, she would have made too!

"The country was charming—yes! And was he acquainted with it? 'Not this part.' Ah, so. And was Monsieur," (she begged pardon for her English), " was he going farther north than themselves?" Their own destination she cleverly avoided naming.

"To Yorkshire! In-deed! It might be for sport, to shoot grouse or partridge—she knew little of these cruel amusements. No! ... ah ... Harrogate was in Yorkshire, was it not; so perhaps his destination was in its environs? Why—was it not droll?—he was actually going there!—and so were they. Could he kindly tell them which hotel he preferred? Strange: they had already written for rooms in the same ... yet, excuse her curiosity, could he possibly be going there for health?"

And so on, and so on; till, despite his reluctance, she had discovered this much which you already know, O reader! and something more; to wit, that his regiment was in India, from whence he had come home on leave, having travelled through little known wilds of Asia, and parts of Russia, in returning; that he had caught a wearisome low fever afterwards, and meant to drink the waters, to regain strength before the Autumn.

If she did not know his name, still she had read the initials on his dressing-bag. And if she did not as yet know that he was a younger son, belonged to a fairly rich and influential old family, and had been pitch-forked into the world when only fresh from a public school, with his education, his commission, and a few hundreds a year—

(besides her ignorance of his idiosyncrasies
before-mentioned)—why, she meant soon to
be informed about them all.

This foreign lady, too, cared about as much
for the unwillingness of the luckless person
.into whose private matters she chose to in-
quire, as might a sleek ferret steadily keeping
its nose to the scent despite repelling bram-
bles, while stealthily following up its victim
to explore the most sacred privacies of his
burrow.

She did not, however, tell him, in her
turn, that she was Mrs. Langton, second
wife of Miles Langton, the old master of
Cherrybank—a pleasant place in one of the
south-western shires. Only she occasionally
put her long fingers, in a creeping, fawning
way, on the arm of the old man beside
her, who sat bent and silent, both hands
clasped on his stick; his locks of hair—
which showed they had once been red by a
faint yellowish hue still lingering in their
whiteness—falling on the collar of his black

coat. Dreamily and immoveably he kept gazing through his spectacles at the dusty carriage-lining opposite him. When she so touched him, however, he would give a nervous start, glance round with painful slowness, and a timid suspicion in his look; then droop his weary head again with the old musing, searching expression.

"We hope the waters may restore my husband's health," was the sole information she graciously volunteered to the now resigned Huntley. "The change will also amuse my daughter during her holidays—is it not so, Ma-belle?"

No answer. Mabel was intently staring at some of Wat's papers, which he had just offered her—a smile on her lips, and her mind evidently far away in some happy reverie.

Mrs. Langton's face changed, and her voice had an unpleasant, cold incisiveness; though she smiled most charmingly, after a peculiar surface fashion.

" Dreaming, as usual. Do you not, then, hear me, *chère petite ?*"

The *chère petite* gave a quick start, mechanically answering, "Yes, Madame;" and then, with her face concealed by the paper from all eyes save Huntley's—of whose observation she was most likely unaware,—gave a look of such fiendish detestation at the head of her unconscious step-mother, that it was all Walter could do to keep from laughing outright.

"What a queer little vixen?" he again said to himself; watching her soft, mobile features resume once more the childishly sulky expression he had first noted. Then at last the train rushed, screaming, puffing, and slackening, into the station at Harrogate.

Dusty and tired, they all got out to seize what of their luggage was visible in the general *mêlée*. Our first acquaintance, Captain Huntley, had soon secured his own, and made his way to their hotel in time to come down for dinner irreproachably dressed in the black and white garb of gentlemen— (and waiters)—in our nineteenth century. His fellow-travellers in the train were not at the *table-d'hôte*, however, as one or two glances around showed; but he felt none the less cheerful for being surrounded by the total strangers who lined two long tables stretching the whole length of the room.

CHAPTER II.

"My hair was golden yellow, and it floated to my shoe ;
  My eyes were like two harebells, bathed in little drops
  of dew."

R. BUCHANAN.

ABOUT three hours later, when a warm darkness was settling down upon the town, the green Stray, and the trees beyond—when sounds of music floated out from lighted rooms through open windows, —a young girl was seated at her dressing-table, in a small bed-room of the hotel, whilst her maid was brushing out a thick mass of beautiful red-gold hair, which seemed to assert itself all the more in loosely-waving rebellion.

"Be quick, Agnes—we are late; and she may come in any moment. Oh! don't get me into fresh disgrace, for I have a punishment task already that will take me two hours to learn to-morrow."

Agnes Hitchcocks, the maid, whom Mabel Langton addressed, only gave a great start, and stared vacantly at the door, with uplifted brush; then, satisfying herself that there was no immediate danger, placidly resumed her occupation.

"La! no, Miss Mabel; she's too busy with your papa. He looks very bad to-night; poor dear gentleman!"

"She would not let me say good night to him—poor papa!" And Mabel, though she began in a tone of suppressed vindictiveness, ended with a sigh.

Hitchcocks, although a remarkably cheerful, good-looking, young woman, of an age, perhaps, slightly over thirty, echoed the. sigh; and gave vent, in a similarly cautious murmur, to some bitter, but almost inaudible, observations relative to "one's own flesh and blood."

Evidently the subject was no new one between them; but, for some reason or other, both maid and little mistress seemed afraid of raising their voices to a natural pitch.

"But if it's only tasks for punishment, I would never mind, Miss Mabel, dear. Why, only last week you were nigh crying because she would teach you nothing herself, nor yet get you masters."

"If the tasks were any use, I should be glad of them; but they are not, and she never hears me say them."

In her heart, Mabel suspected that her step-mother was not very capable in her teaching, and gave a great sigh; then her mind reverted to the stranger, and she observed, in confidence, with an aggrieved tone:

"There was a gentleman in the train to-day, Agnes; he came here too. He

was talking to her a good deal." (Miss
Hitchcocks's nose sloped a degree more
upwards than even nature had intended,
with a secret contemptuous enmity against
whoever had so ranged himself on the side
of the oppressor.) "What a fright he must
have thought me, with my hair down, and
that old short frock!"

"I *have* let down the tuck in your silk,
missy, dear; but, Lord love us! don't let
her see it, for any sake," returned Hitchcocks, in an awe-struck but delighted whisper; unable to keep any longer to herself a
secret with such a pleasant flavour of
wrong-doing. "And what was he like?"

No answer; so her attendant, who had not
been born and bred at Cherrybank, and been
Mabel's little nursemaid first, and her close
attendant—indeed (as she herself considered)
her principal care-taker—ever since, without
learning Miss Langton's proud little ways,
perceived her curiosity was resented, so
adroitly continued :

"To think that, all these years, you shouldn't have seen a single strange soul; excepting your papa and your old school-master, as used to come before her day!— Hardly been out of our own fields ; as one may say."

Confused as this sentence seems, it meant that Mr. Langton's absences from home, for years past, had made him indeed little more than a stranger.   To the mind of Agnes she herself and the middle-aged butler were Mabel's humble friends; and her only ones, as for a long time they had alone been her faithful guardians.

" It will just be like coming out into the world from a convent, as me and Mr. Bennet were saying the other night in the room ; and he and I agreed as we'd keep our rispective diries all this month and note down all that 'appens to both of us; taking other names for each other like—as seeming less vulgar."   Her young mistress's lips parted with a little smile of amusement; a secret

satisfaction to her attached attendant, whose
constant effort was "to cheer her up a bit."
"Mr. Bennet thinks Madam of late so fear-
somely like the white lady,—the ghost down
our lane." Miss Hitchcocks's voice became
even more low; and she glanced cautiously
round. "Well, well; his is to begin with to-
day's date, and, 'The family is gone!' . . . My
names—" continued this attendant nymph;
fixing her eyes for inspiration on the top of
the small iron bed—"my names is not so
clear in my head; for, seeing I've so many
ideas, it's harder to choose; whilst he has
only one at a time, if as many. But I've
already two pages wrote about our leave
taking. Mine begins, 'As I sat by the
pantry-window——' "

"What were you doing there, Agnes?"

The unexpected nature of this attack so
took aback that unusually confident personage that for a moment or so she was dumb;
then, recovering herself, answered glibly,
with conscious virtue,

" Mr. Bennet was so good as to sharpen me some pencils, Miss Langton; being handier than pens and ink. And it's not my usual practice neither, to——"

" A-a-ah! You are pulling my hair," and Mabel put up both hands with a little scream. (Had she seen an opening door reflected in the looking-glass, though there was neither creak nor sound of footfall; and through the aperture a face appearing which would have suited a pale abbess, with downcast eyes and thin lips, gliding her rounds of cruel, unceasing supervision over warmer-hearted, evil-unsuspecting sisters ?). Anyhow, both gave a guilty start as a voice—which somehow always made poor, wicked little Mabel's flesh creep and writhe with hatred—said, icily and distinctly; each word falling one by one like a slight sprinkle of hail-stones: "Not in bed? Heetchcocks, you may go. Will you in future remember, Mademoiselle, that conversation with your inferiors is *défendue* . . .

I trust you will not dislike the dark."

The solitary candle was blown out, and the door closed upon this parting sneer; leaving the abashed culprit alone.

She was not without consoling resources, however. In a few seconds she had noiselessly locked herself in; then, flinging aside the curtains and opening wide the window, she knelt down with both elbows on the sill; her chin resting on her small brown hands. Wrapped in white with her glory of hair she might have seemed like a child-saint framed, not in gilding, but in the stone-work round the window, were any eyes in the garden below to look up and espy that small, dreamy, upturned face—despite the deep shadows of the warm-scented August night. For there was only a sickle moon in its faint, first quarter, that seemed averting its face from earth.

Were there such eyes ? There was—at least—a spot of red glow like the tip of a cigar, near those laurels skirting the walls;

and no footsteps could be heard on the grass.

But Mabel was looking far away—past the hotel-garden with its flower-beds and railings—its scents of sleeping mignonette and carnations—out over the open Stray, where was a cooler, faint night-breeze—beyond the lights of the town in the hollow; almost beyond the tremulous haze of that greyish azure sky-vault, which would be so warm and beautiful a blue, did the darkness not veil it with soberer shades. She was in an enchanted land, where everything was strange and new, and therefore beautiful.

How different from the terrible solitude of Cherrybank, with its dell and woods; which, though dear, had no longer, like this country, the charm of being unexplored!

She heard music too. There were the strains of a valse floating upwards,—broad gleams from lighted windows were thrown on the grass, but sometimes obscured by quick, flitting shadows. And the stealing charm of those novel sounds; the wafts of flower scents; the enwrapping darkness; the exciting though vague sense of dreams fulfilled, and of seeing the world at last!—at last!—(she who had only just once before left that home where she had been reared by the servants in loneliness and strict seclusion),—all made the passionate, hot heart of this motherless, uncared-for child expand with a delicious vague delight; while her pulses quickened and the white wrapper rose and fell with her deep-drawn breaths.

Only sixteen; and an utter child in mind, as she was still unusually so in appearance! And yet to-night she felt older—felt as if life were opening before her,—that some change *must* surely happen, different from the former utter solitude, or from the bitter presence of her step-mother, who was now so hard; so smilingly merciless! She was almost like a caged tigress in her wild, young heart this night. One whose free nature had not yet been subdued by prison bars, waiting and watching every chance that they would at last be broken, and let her taste the sweets of wild liberty again.

Voices broke the night spell.

It was only two of the chamber-maids and an attentive waiter playfully wrangling beyond the garden-wall, on that white strip of road she could just see beneath those tall poplar trees at the servants' entrance. But she was awakened from the dream; her head disappeared in interior darkness, and only the empty window-frame remained.

A minute afterwards Walter Huntley flung the end of his cigar somewhere among the dark laurels, and turned away with an inward laugh at his own absurdity in staring so long furtively at the dim outline of a little school-girl's head. Next, taking a final look at the weather, he mused whether the doctor, whom he meant to consult to-morrow, would advise him to try for prolonged leave; then thought he would

have a look at the billiard-room, and perhaps play a game or two before turning in to
bed.

CHAPTER III.

"Along this rock I'll lie,
  With face turned upward to the sky;
  A dreamy numbness glows within' my brain;
  It is not joy, and is not pain."

R. BUCHANAN.

ON the afternoon of the next day, Walter Huntley was trying to kill the slow time.

He was lying down at the foot of Birk Crag, under the partial shade of a big boulder; seeing only, through his half-closed eyes, rocks, a mountain ash, and a strip of sky across which a gorged rook was slowly flapping with hoarse caws. Other people were away on expeditions that hot afternoon, either at shady Bolton, or nearer hand at Plumpton Rocks, or exploring Knaresborough's ruined castle; but he knew no one at Harrogate, and consoled himself by reflecting that he had come strictly for health,—not for pleasure.

And he had much to think over as he lay there half dreaming; in fact, whether or not he should make this Autumn a turning-point in his life, or go on yet awhile in the old tracks. His doctor had, that morning, pronounced him able to go back to India in October; yet feared its climate would hardly be good for his constitution, tried as was the latter by his late long travels.

What then? He had only stayed on in the army, for the last year or so, from habit and strong liking for his brother-officers; yet wishing for, and looking forward to, a change of life; since early ardour had died of inaction, and powers, and modes of thought, that could not be freely developed in his present profession, had grown up within him. He cared little for general society; he was sick to death of country quarters, and of a constant peace-horizon; he wanted hard work, took all he could, yet found it mostly husks, unsatisfying to mental hunger; and his mind, altered and expanded, demanded other labour in the world.

Ambition of a quiet, moderate sort had grown up in him—late, yet all the more lasting.

During the last four years or so, he had satisfied his honest soul by taking up various studies with thorough conscientiousness; scientific, some of them, but mostly on politics, especially certain great measures, then looming in the future; for Parliament was the goal of his present ambition, and the starting-point of future plans.

It was now almost a tradition that the borough of Lufton had always returned a Huntley; and that every Huntley was a Liberal. Lufton was a market-town; and theirs was, perhaps, the greatest family in those parts. Walter's elder brother—himself lazy, rich, married, and devoted to his duties as a master of hounds—kept urging him to take the seat their old uncle was considered only to hold for him.

Yet Wat hesitated. He loved the old man, and knew that the latter, though no speaker, and but a muddle-headed politician, still wished to keep his pride of place, despite gout, one session more. And Walter also doubted whether he could well afford the more expensive life; for though the one of all the Huntleys whom they all most gladly welcomed, he was by far the poorest. No legacies had fallen to him; since everyone believed that the fortune his mother *must* inherit would be his. But his mother had died without inheritance, and the said fortune had enriched a new-born little heir, so he was still "poor Wat," but good-humoured as ever.

"India, it must be . . ." he dreamily thought. With his arms beneath his head, he was nearly asleep. That rock overhead becomes a beetling crag, shading him from the tropical heat of the glowing east. Did not palms crown its barren summit instead of a mere tuft of British fern; while the drowsy murmuring in his ears must be the sound of a far-off torrent—not the tiny beck, springing from the hillside, his waking senses had seen?

What was that noise above him?

A scramble!—a grating, descending rush! —a stoppage—and—a sudden breaking away of an overhanging sod which sent a rasping shower of earth, grass, and pebbles full on the face of our dreamer! "What, in the name of all that is startling——?" He had gained his feet, and, clearing the earth from his face and eyes, was staring up to see the cause in a very few seconds.

Overhead, and clinging only to the burnt, slippery turf just above the boulder, like a wild, frightened kitten taking refuge up a tree, was a terrified young girl,—looking down at the fall below with fear, yet set determination, on her white face. Both her hands were grasping for a hold on the short grass that broke from her fingers as she slipped downward!—one foot was desperately planted against a slight projection; but the other in trying a treacherous sod had broken it away, causing Wat's earthy libation. And sheer below that foot the rock sloped down to him!

"You can't hold there a minute longer! Listen—get both feet on that stone, then turn and jump and I'll catch you," he cried; taking in the whole danger at a glance, and instinctively stretching up his arms, though she was so high above him.

"I won't! Go away—I shall jump by myself," in a tone in which alarm was overcome by shyness and pride.

"Don't, child, for heaven's sake! you'll be killed to a dead certainty——"

The grass was slipping away from her sore fingers now! Another moment, and she must jump after some fashion, or risk falling in a heap. Her dress gave one parting rent from a bramble as she turned, and—mad child that she was!—sprang with one reckless leap into the air, so as to light on the ground clear of him.

But, quick as herself, he had guessed the intention, and springing to that side, caught her—luckily for her neck; yet could not prevent her coming heavily to the ground.

Jarred himself by the force of the shock, he watched anxiously, after helping her to a seat on a big stone, to see whether she was not greatly shaken, while she held her head tight between both hands. Just as he was getting frightened, and glancing round for water, she looked up.

"Oh! It is you—is it?" said the rather childish heroine, slowly, as if bewildered; putting down her hands, but eyeing him with an air that seemed to imply his interference was solely in fault.

Much relieved, Wat expressed his conviction to little Miss Langton that it was himself.

"How do you know my name?—I don't know yours," she asked naïvely, but with a slight air of haughtiness that could not conceal evident shyness.

"I read yours in the visitors' book. Mine is Captain Huntley," he answered, with kindly re-assurance in his manner.

Clearly, as Mab acknowledged with an inward sigh, it was her duty to thank this stranger; and despite the formidable nature of the task, she acquitted herself of it—somewhat stammeringly, yet prettily enough.

But Wat could not help smiling; his fancy was so tickled by the unconscious way in which she drew backward, glowering child-like from under her eyelashes, as if to hint that gratitude must not induce her to lower dignity—and it seemed so absurd to be afraid of *him*!

"You have no idea how you frightened me by appearing so suddenly overhead—my nerves are still quite shaken!" he craftily said.

She looked up with such sharp suspicion, however, that it upset his gravity, and he broke into a hearty laugh.

Her assumption of dignity changed to doubtfulness, but in another second that too faded from her soft young face; glad reaction after fright asserted itself; and she joined in his mirth so naturally, reminding him of the happy gurgle of some full-throated wild bird, that a good understanding was at once established between them.

"Whereabouts are Mr. and Mrs. Langton? Did you run away; for, if so, I trust they are not following exactly in your footsteps?"

"What nonsense! Madame,—my stepmother, I mean—never takes me with her." (Wat rightly guessed the term was used to avoid that one sacred to her own mother). "She went to walk with poor papa a little, and I feel lonely somehow among many people; so I wandered down here to get some ferns, if any rare ones could be found."

"And this is the end of your search! But I am sorry to see your hands all bleeding and bruised inside. Suppose you wash the earth out of the cuts, at least?"

So, as her new charge assented, they gravely proceeded a few yards downhill to a tiny beck sparkling over its gravelly bed; a clear little hillside runlet, that would hardly seem a river to any minnow, save one of the most contracted ideas; and Wat felt, for all the world, as if he were a nine-year old boy again,—going to fish for sticklebacks by help of two pieces of twine and a couple of crooked pins, with his little sister, who had died before she was even eight.

Down sat Mabel, tailor-wise, one elbow leant upon a tussock of grass; and so, bending forward, let the clear water sparkle over one brown hand, small, but purposeful; no mere plump Hebe's; then lazily washed its fellow. Somehow, in her, the attitude was neither unladylike nor ungraceful, as it would have appeared in another

schoolgirl; it seemed only unconventional—
like herself; and that small figure, free in
curves and action as any classic nymph's,
swayed as she pleased.

Walter, meanwhile, stretched beside her,
with his arms crossed on a flat grey-stone,
first silently watched her; then amused
himself by vainly trying to stop her supply
of water with both hands.

His innocent entertainment over—since she
now began painfully endeavouring to cut out
several thorns that had worked deeply into
her ill-used fingers,—he listened, with an
amused, good-humoured smile on his kindly
though ugly face, to her gay chatter about
the whole accident—when she had slid first;
and how glad she had really felt on seeing
him down below.

"Do take them out, please; they *won't*
come for me," she suddenly said, giving him
her knife as if prepared to endure any pain;
and showing her sores as simply as any child
will desire a grown person to wait upon it,

who, instinct whispers, is easily tyrannised over.

He, for his part, took hold of them just as naturally (though no less deferentially than had she been a fairy princess); and, having extracted the thorns, resisted any temptation to keep those pretty, hurt hands even one half second longer than was just necessary.

"What an ugly head that is, carved upon your stick!" she said—for her eyes had been wandering.

"Do you think so? A brother-officer gave it, because it was so like me; and whenever I meet a plainer man than myself, I am bound to pass it on to him."

His light-hearted merriment, that always accompanied a remark upon his want of personal attraction, made her again laugh too.

"But was it *fair* to call you so ugly?" she said, with kindly afterthought, looking at him shyly; but evidently thinking no one

could object to an impartial analysis of what
was, after all, no work of his own, but a
mere freak of nature.

It was a very honest face—one you
would have known, in any part of the
world, with a well-pleased recognition, to
be English. A square head and open
forehead, fair hair, of no particular shade;
a reddish moustache, and a fresh, sanguine,
but very sunburnt complexion. All this
was well enough; but not so was an
unsightly scar passing over one high cheek-
bone of his rough-hewn visage, from the
corner of an eyebrow, where it contracted
into strange wrinkles whenever (as was
very often the case) he laughed and looked
cheerily out at the world from those
sunken, but merry and truthful, light-blue
eyes.

There were various rumours afloat—and
all of them rather flattering ones—as to its
origin. Some folk averred it was caused
by a fall at some celebrated race or other—

an unusual event, since his fame as the
winner of certain racing victories was
long talked of in mess-rooms; but, in
truth, it dated from old school-days, when a
big bully had over-punished a little boy—a
cheat; and Wat, interfering in this un-
romantic cause, got soundly thrashed for his
pains, and was flung against a door-scraper.

Then as to his nose, it was one which,
though depressed where it left the protection
of his forehead, re-asserted itself vigorously
in the centre, and was wide-blown—not to
say broad—at the end.

Such was poor Wat's plain face; only with
an addition of honesty and manliness in its
expression, not easily to be defined, but
always unhesitatingly trusted.

"Well—he was right, was he not?"
laughed Wat, as Miss Mabel ended her
short scrutiny and dropped her eyes—since
truth compelled a hard verdict, but she
felt really reluctant and sorry to give it.

"Well, perhaps! it is not exactly what

some people only like, certainly. Never mind—perhaps you'll get used to it, like me," and she gave him a comforting look of full fellow-sympathy; then, suddenly changing her tone, added, "You will soon find, however, that I am not only ugly, but perfidious; and as to manners—a savage!"

There was a flash of tears in her eyes; though she tried to twist her mobile features into a little scowl, so like her strange grimace in the train that Wat felt certain without a doubt that she was quoting some taunt—perhaps even her smooth-tongued stepmother's,—which had sorely wounded her innocent girlish vanities. He looked at her pityingly, and with kindness; in his heart admiring the creamy complexioned, soft, small face, with its firm chin and pouting crimson lips; though her glorious hair was brushed off it with trying tightness and twisted into plaits.

"What a baby you are to mind such

nonsense !" he found himself saying, as if he were a good-natured elder brother.

"A baby! Pray do you know how old I am?" she asked; flaring out at once in quick anger, but with great dignity.

"Have not the slightest idea," answered Wat, with alarmed politeness. "Fourteen, or—*perhaps*—fifteen, I should say."

"I shall be seventeen my *next* birthday!"

"Is it possible. But—might I ask—how long ago was your last one?"

That was unkind; and her face fell.

"Two months ago—but all the same, I am quite old, you see."

And as he assented gravely, "Quite old; not a doubt of it;" being too good-hearted to ruffle her new-fledged plumes, she felt perfectly happy.

"But will Mr. and Mrs. Langton not be uneasy at your wandering away alone?" he went on; made suddenly mindful of society's decorum.

"Why should they? I have always gone alone since I can remember, and now I am only better able to take care of myself."

"But," he gently answered; searching in his mind as to what he should say, since he himself loved better to think that their own sweetness and dignity, rather than mere forms and usages, should hedge in women; "but most people grow so much fonder of their daughters every year that, when these are as old as you, they do not like to miss them from their side."

A dark shadow came upon her face, where every passing change was mirrored, plain as clouds in a clear mountain tarn. "Ah! So most parents are like that, are they?" ("But not all," she said in her heart, which swelled—"not all!")

However, she rose up to go, looking round. The sun had sloped more westward, and its golden rays kissed her bared head; for her hat hung from her careless fingers. She seemed like a fresh innocent daisy to the man beside her; a yellow-headed daisy, white and pure and strong, if small; faintly tinged with rosier colour.

He went back with her, of course, since it seemed very necessary for some one to look after her. Yes, indeed! otherwise there was no knowing what further scrapes she might get into; and he glanced at her with a little shake of the head, yet withal an indulgent smile.

For her, she soon grew gleeful again, and talked to him all the way back, as if he were a big playfellow—at times with a laughable little air of protection, as if feeling her sex superior; or as if accustomed to exercise a kindly but imperious sway over those around her. But, as both recognised two figures far off, walking slowly upon the grassy Stray, her face grew troubled and hesitating; her feet plainly slackened.

" Cheer up," something prompted Wat to whisper, in encouragement, as they drew nearer; "Mrs. Langton looks quite smilingly at you."

But she only gave her head an all but imperceptible shake. She would rather have seen her step-mother frowning than gazing at both with that cool, inquiring, most irritating smile.

"Madame, I had an accident," she said, plucking up courage and going quickly forward. "I went wandering off alone, and fell down a steep place; and this gentleman picked me up—and—and——"

There she stopped, stammering. Who *could* go on under that cold, mocking smile?

"And you tore your frock; and made yourself a fright of disorder to behold! Look at her only, dear sir!" said Mrs. Langton, with an amused air; while the old man, who required the most fastidious neatness in those around him, turned away his head in great annoyance.

Then Huntley interfered, and explained

to the lady,—who very graciously recognised him,—in what real danger the little girl
had been—and all because she was trying
to gather ferns for her father.

"Have you got them, Mabel?" asked the
old man, with something that was almost
eagerness in his trembling voice; then
looked sadly disappointed, as she had to
answer, no.

"But at least she tried her best, and was
hurt," he muttered to himself—"Yes, she
did—little Mabel."

"You had better go to your own room,
and repose yourself, dear child," said Mrs.
Langton, calmly; and then, with her most
engaging manner, she pressed Huntley to
spend that evening in their sitting-room.

He accepted; and she and her husband
continued their slow saunter.

But the poor old man was now disturbed;
and his weak nerves seemed to sicken and
revolt at the presence he could not escape
from—half a step behind; yet always close.

He who had been so used to muse in happy solitude—who had always avoided woman-kind. As she dutifully held an umbrella over his bent head, passers-by perhaps admired that air of meek devotion; but the rustling of her garments over the grass was almost unendurable to her feeble, weak-brained old husband, in whose eyes the very sun-light seemed darker for that baleful influence. With a great effort he tried to break the fascination.

"Mabel—my daughter—was hurt," he said, stopping to face her. "Why do you not see after her? Her governess—her governess—was more attentive."

For a moment his wife was thunder-struck; then she looked at him with a steady gaze, under which he quailed a little, and uneasily averted his feeble eyes; but she only said, "As you wish," then left him.

"Her governess!" Ah! old dotard! she would pay him off for that taunt.

(For she alone had been Mab's governess; and six months ago she had persuaded the old man to marry her.) Yet he seemed to have forgotten her identity with that governess; he could hardly be dissembling? He would have received a worse punishment than the finely cruel one she still designed for him, had she guessed that his once subtle mind, now deteriorated, through disease of the brain, into cunning, at times simulated such a want of memory as to exercise a safe childish revenge upon her.

An hour afterwards the old man shambled into their sitting-room, weak and weary. He longed for shade, but the blinds were up, and the setting sun poured full upon his eyes, pained and throbbing, as were his temples, for want of the umbrella she had taken away from him. Where was this new strange woman—his wife—who generally refreshed him with a cup of tea, and placed cushions in his arm-chair? No cushions to be seen—they were carefully hidden away;

and he tried to hide himself from the draught and glare on a hard chair in one corner, where he leant his white head against the wall.

At last—at last—he could hear the rustle of her dress, and felt she was sitting opposite, looking at him. Against his will he must unclose his eyes and see her; then her cold, quietly angry voice jarred upon him. " You are awake, Monsieur—will you listen to me? . . . You know when you married me that I offered still to teach Mabel; but each day she grows wilder, ruder, and more disobedient. No one would think her your daughter! She will *never* be a lady! I have come to tell you, you must get a governess, or send her to school; and pay a great deal too—no one would take such a charge without *much* money!"

"No, no. It is expensive, and I am not rich. Keep her at home," he muttered; and at that a little contemptuous smile curled her lips, for she thought him a miser;

and so he was in some ways, but not in this.

"Then you must punish her yourself, for I can no longer endure such persecution. See her an hour ago, wild and torn! *Juste ciel!* What can strangers think of her? It was not even respectable—it was not the appearance of a girl of good family."

" My ferns—for me," the poor old father stammeringly tried to plead; but, with a sudden movement that startled him, she forced him to look full in her eyes.

" *That was a lie!*" not mincing the word; but with a (to him) terrible emphasis. Then, as a faint red flush suffused his worn pale features, and he sat upright with an effort, she went on rapidly: " Yes, it revolts you; I do not wonder. Where were her proofs? Had she the ferns? No, indeed! Instead of staying quietly in her room to learn justly-inflicted tasks, she escapes, as if she were a wild beast caged instead of an English miss, and was rightly punished. I suspected all; and

I was right—she told you not the truth."

"Then I will not speak to her if she comes into the room; I do not wish to see her," said the old man, with quivering lips. She was his only child, his own flesh and blood, and she had transgressed the creed he held most sacred!

"You will not punish her yourself?"

"No, no. I cannot bear to speak to her about it. Do as you think best."

And she, well-pleased, for she had rightly counted on his answer, soothed and quieted him; pulled down the blinds and brought his tea. Her voice was soft and low now, and she supplied his every want. When he looked at her tasteful, neutral-tinted dress, his eye was perforce pleased; never shocked as by poor little Mab's ill-fitting attire.

Upstairs, the latter had been waiting alone ever since she went indoors, expecting some evil doom or other, from old experience—a boding confirmed by Hitchcocks, who, tearfully summoning her to Madame's room, whispered to her charge that something bad was surely coming, for "missus was a-smiling to herself."

Then began a lecture such as during the last months had maddened, almost past all endurance, the warm-hearted girl, whom no one,—never certainly her governess,—had ever so spoken to before. It was calm and slow, but every word stung; and as the wretched victim stood with folded hands near the door, unnerved already by the long wait, as her stepmother well knew, she felt, in spite of trying hard to be controlled, that soon the storm within her must burst.

Madame took a curious but real pleasure in trying how long she could make this torture last, without maddening the sufferer to the utmost; but at last she grew impatient. She had already from every point taunted the girl with her adventure; and though to her face she could accuse her of nothing worse than the behaviour of a hoyden, she in-geniously added to that every past transgression for weeks back. Again and again she satirically implied that Mabel Langton was not a lady; bah!—had not even the mind, far less manners, of one! This scoff of being unladylike came from a mine of insult she already knew well how to work; for no other so wounded the proud, romantic little heart, shrinking from base things, passionately longing to be pure and high. True, Madame was not at first surprised by her conduct—brought up like any peasant girl as she was among ploughmen and *canaille*. But had she not had Madame's own example and teaching for a year and a half; and was she one whit less boorish? None could now doubt that it was in her own temperament; and as all could see her manners were not inherited from her father, she thus laid her dead mother open to the suspicion of transmitting to her daughter such uncouth ways and love of low company, like that of her maid and the vile old dependants.

Even that the child bore, though her

heart swelled and her knees shook, and she
could hardly bear it. But when Madame
added that her father had been so disgusted
with her appearance, he would not look at
her if she came down—her father!—whose
approval was the one thing on earth she
yearned for, and so seldom—alas! so seldom
—gained, then her wild wrath and indignation burst forth like a torrent. Choking
back her sobs, she accused Madame to her
face of making mischief between herself
and her only parent. Instinct seemed to
supply her want of knowledge of what had
passed, and the temper that since childhood
had never been checked, blazed so fiercely that even the Frenchwoman was over-
borne by its torrent. Pale with anger, she
ordered the girl at once to her own room;
and then the key was turned upon her.

Two hours passed; Mab had sobbed
herself out, and tears had extinguished the
hot fire in her heart. Now she sat on the
floor by the open window, looking wearily

out across the twilight common, hugging her knees in her bitterness. She heard noises down below in the house; the dinner-hour was long past, and being healthy and active, she was hungry, but hardly expected (from former experiences), to be given much food. At last the door was softly unlocked and opened, and Mrs. Langton glided in, with one small slice of bread on a plate, and a glass of spring water.

"Here is your dinner and your punishment, Mabel," she calmly uttered; and no saint could have looked down more impassionately at the girl. "*I* have already forgiven you, and I can but trust (though it is unlikely) that you will become truly penitent and more Christian. For me, you may come down if you wish; though your father —you know what he said."

"I will not go down—I shall not trouble him."

And the door closed once more.

The window was open, and the next moment, with one passionate throw, the bread was flung out, and fell far below on the grass. Again poor, angry little Mab crouched down, and laid her head upon the sill. Another long, long hour passed, and the tea-gong had sounded; while the shadows outside fell darkly and thick, and she had grown hungry once more. A small rough terrier came out from the side-door, and sniffed for a moment at the bread below, then turned away in contempt.

Mab wished heartily she could only get it back.

She felt ashamed of herself, but she stole to the plate and ate a few crumbs still left upon it, and drank her water. Then she heard Agnes Hitchcocks whispering at the keyhole, and sniffling a little, being evidently in tears. "Oh, Miss Mabel!—oh, my poor dear!—they've called me to my supper, but 'ow could I ever enjoy my food and you fasting? *I'll fast too!*"

Clearing her voice, Mab tried to assure

her faithful maid that, upon the whole, she rather enjoyed it; so Hitchcocks let herself be persuaded not to do martyrdom for her mistress's sake. "She has on her best gown, the green and grey, has Madam; and she has got the strange gentleman you met to-day in there for the evening," was her last whispered news.

That was the final stroke. Mabel got into bed then, and hid her head under the bed-clothes, as if trying to shut out all her troubles with the shadows and the darkening twilight, which she was sick of watching. She had been dreaming and thinking for days of the new life she would lead on this visit—the strange adventures and wonderful happiness that would surely gild the fresh page. Why, it was even a wonder to leave home—to see all the gay young folk in the great world; while her foolish little mind had imagined so many possible deliverances from her cruel dragon of a step-mother, like fairy-tales eked out with memories of

queer old-world romances.   And this was
the end of the first day !

Even that nice ugly friend she had made,
towards whom she already felt some of
the affection she bestowed on her rough-
coated water-dog at home, was downstairs
with Madame; and he would of course learn
how wicked she was, and look at her
sorrowfully ever after, even as did all that
lady's acquaintances.

As it happened, Huntley was asking for
her at that very moment.   Mrs. Langton
had taken the service he had rendered their
daughter as the ground for making his
closer acquaintance, and was now conversing
in the dim twilight in low undertones with
him, while poor old Miles dozed.   Wat felt
she was bent on captivating him ; but had
none the less an aversion for her, and wished heartily for his fair-haired playfellow.
" Our little girl is in bed.   She was too
wild and shy to come in when you were
here.   She is such a mere child—only just

going into her teens; so pray forgive her
rudeness, for my sake. Ah, monsieur, I
have sad trouble; a step-mother's life is one
of many mortifications."

As she ended, sighing gently, and looking
away, Walter felt inclined to doubt her
strict veracity. He thought that night with
warmed feelings of the lonely little maiden
who had so strangely made his acquaintance.
But she was weaving dreams, in her sleep,
of far other heroes than such as he: of a
knight of knights, stately, and tall, and gal-
lant!—a dark, fierce, handsome warrior,
whose wild prowess and daring deeds swept
away all thoughts of the plain, prosaic Wat
Huntley she had met by Birk Crag that
day.

CHAPTER IV.

"The woods drone
A drowsy song that in its utterance dies;
And the dim voice of indolent herds floats by
With slow, luxurious calm. The runnel hath
Its tune beneath the trees. The insect throng,
Drunk with the wine of Summer, dart and dance
In mazy play; and through the woodlands swell
The tender trembles of the ring-dove's dole."

C. NEWTON.

AS far back as Mabel Langton could remember, even to the most hazily-
golden of childhood's memories, almost all
the events of her short sixteen years had
passed at Cherrybank, her home. Far, far
behind in that dim time she seemed to recall
a beautiful pale-faced mother, always sad,
always gentle. She was nearly certain she

could remember clearly her step-sister's marriage—(for the first Mrs. Langton had been a widow with one daughter). Or was it only that Agnes had so often told her how she—a toddling, yellow-haired baby—had sobbed because a certain hale, ruddy-faced, but grey-haired gentleman, who seemed very old to her infant mind, was taking away her dear Maud?

Little Mab had been only up to her mother's knee then; but, in the three or four years that followed, she had grown big enough to romp with her faithful dog; to watch Dolly milking the cows, both morning and evening; or to hide among the green pea-rows, or deep down in the seeded grass of the meadow, that almost closed over her head in a delightful nest, while poor Agnes searched vainly for the charge who ought to have been in her cot. And all those months her mother drooped day by day, pining away in that ever calm, monotonous, loveless home.

In those days it seemed as if she could
hardly recall seeing her father, except at
stray times, when the awe and reverence
for his mysterious learning, taught to the
child by the poor heart-sick mother, laid
the foundation for the secret, dim worship
Mabel afterwards cherished for him.

Then that mother died. Even now
Mabel never thought of her but with
longing regret for the sweet-eyed saint
who—had her suffering on earth been
prolonged—would surely have saved her
child from that growth of strong-rooted
wickednesses which, alas! Madame declared
to be ineradicable. For, like many another,
our little heroine ascribed her fallings-away
far more readily to her circumstances than
to her inner self.

Afterwards, for years, memory brought
back nothing but the dim outline of herself
living there,—always alone! She grew older
and stronger, and a little bigger; but nothing else changed in the low-built, gabled

old house, looking down into the dell of the Nye, at its very foot; while straight in front rose up the grand old woods that the moss-covered park-walls jealously bounded.

Spring and Autumn, Summer and Winter, her little figure alone wandered, at sunrise, through the dew-wet meadows; or lay in the woods at midday, gazing up at the pale green, fresh leaves that began to chequer thickly the great hemisphere of the sapphire sky overhead; or again, with her dog, bounded through great heaps of brown, rustling leaves, piled up by the swirl of some wild, wintry gale.

It was strange of her father to leave the child without guardians or friends of her own station, in the utter seclusion of Cherrybank, with but three old servants; taught only, in the afternoons, by a poor, aged, crack-brained scholar, once an usher. But Miles Langton had always been strange. Till late in life he had buried himself down there, far from men, only caring for his scientific studies; and now (was it because of his wife's death ?—none knew) the place was hateful to him.

Most of the year he was away, travelling on expeditions that had some addition to scientific knowledge in view; coming home for a short visit in Winter, when his child hardly ever entered the rooms where he shut himself up day and night. But to her imagination he was a Humboldt—a Newton; far too learned and great—with eyes that were always striving to read the secrets of the stars, and to penetrate the hidden mysteries of the earth—to see the ignorant but loving little daughter, who looked up to him with such humble awe and reverence deep in her heart.

So she alone was the small mistress of Cherrybank, and she made her authority felt. Why, each Spring had she not designed some wonderful arbour, or rock-house, or Robinson Crusoe's cave-dwelling in the woods, and passed the Summer

working at its completion herself, with
help of the old deaf and dumb man she
made the gardener cede as her own especial
labourer? With what surprise the family
dependants watched the rapid growth of her
studies, and the way she would devour the
dusty pages of strange old books she had
disinterred from the dark library!

She was her father's own child for learning, they used to whisper, nodding to each
other.

And then she had such rides! Who
could feel anything but glad, galloping
on some Autumn day through that grand
south-western country, with a haze over the
thick, deep-hearted woods, and a gleam on
the great far-off, ever-washing sea, while a
strange-scented aroma of moist, rich earth
came up from the steaming fields; deep
banks of rich red soil on either side the
network of lanes, and high above them
rankly luxuriant hedgerows, all tangled
with blackthorn, and bramble, and bracken,

yellow-pink with honeysuckle, golden with
dying fern; at other times belled with hya-
cinths, or full of white and purple violets,
proud Lords-and-Ladies; or again all over-
grown with traveller's-joy, looking, with its
fluffy grey seeds in Autumn, as if the sheep
had left a tribute of wool on those inter-
woven tendrils.

Nearly a fortnight, perhaps, after Huntley's
arrival at Harrogate, he was reading one
afternoon on a bench against the house-wall,
in a quiet spot he had chosen; for the
volume was one which needed all his attention. In front was a shaded plot of
grass, sometimes used by croquet-players,
but now deserted; while just behind was an
open window—that of the large drawing-
room it is true,—but he had glanced in
and seen that the polished floor and big
sofas were vacant and deserted. After
more than an hour, during which no sound
disturbed him, he let drop the book with a
yawn, and turned his head—then gave a

slight start, for not a yard behind him, and curled up in the window-seat, with her eyes fixed upon a book also, was Miss Mab.

"Miss Langton! You there—why, how long were you behind me, and how was it I never heard a sound?"

"I have been here almost as long as you were," she answered, hardly deigning to raise her eyelids. "And of course, when I saw that you were reading, I knew better than to interrupt you; mamma taught me years ago never to disturb papa, and I never do."

"But I *might* have preferred your society —it is quite possible," laughed Wat, whose knowledge and liking of the little lady had made some strides during the intervening time; and who saw she was in a pet, for some reason or other.

"No, no; you did not want me at all. Only—the pity of it is that perhaps my father may. He will be tired, I know, with the long drive Madame is taking him; and I might be of use." The reproach in her sweet, fresh young voice, that tried hard not to sound vexed, and the half-pout, half an effort at womanly dignity, puzzled him.

"Look here," he said, in good-natured coaxing. "You are not pleased—I don't know why. You like to be open and honest—so do I. Tell us all about it."

"Well, you must know, I was longing to drive with him, but Madame said I must stay at home instead, because you had promised to keep my fingers out of mischief, by making me gum in and arrange all your new ferns. I said I was old enough for you to say 'please;' and then she grew very angry, and said an awkward child was not to give herself grown-up airs ; and that you were her friend, and might say to me what you pleased."

Wat felt astonished, for he remembered telling Mrs. Langton, in answer to some passing inquiry, that he meant to have a good read by himself, and had feared that,—in his wish to escape from the companionship he thought she might possibly inflict upon him,— he had seemed misanthropic.

"It is strange, your stepmother did press me to-day to send the ferns to your sitting-room, saying she would arrange them for me; but I dislike so much giving ladies any trouble, I just thought I should do them myself—if possible. Of course your name was never mentioned; I should have thought it an impertinence to venture on such a request."

"Then she was making a fool of me! I should have managed to go somehow, for his sake, but that I thought you did want me," she cried, springing from the sofa, and looking at him with passionate tears in her eyes. She had been deluded, outwitted! Her poor old father had asked for her company, yet, after only some few struggles, she had given way to Madame, believing Huntley did want her assistance; and to her frank child's mind it seemed only fair to do him

what good service she could, in return for
that he had done for her.

And then to find he had not even wanted
her! Luckily, Wat understood a good deal
of it.

"Stay, stay!" he cried, jumping over the
window-sill, and arresting her midway in the
room, as she was in flight, by seizing her
hands. "I thought you were too old and
too wise not to give everyone a chance of
explaining away little misunderstandings.
We have both been made fools of, if you
like; but I have lost most;—the whole last
hour, when I should have liked nothing better than a talk with you."

She was the most forgiving little personage in the world, and, above all things,
fair and honest. There was no coquetry in
the matter, for to her fearless inexperience
all men, as yet, seemed her equals, and
their friendship as possible as that of man
with man. So, being sorry for both herself
and him, in having been mutually disappoint-

ed, she let herself be persuaded to go back, and both discussed the affair.

" What can your stepmother have meant?" said Huntley, more perplexed than she knew. For though many little things he had already noticed made him suspect that Mrs. Langton was but superficially versed in the rules of good society, still to send the girl to spend an afternoon, perhaps, alone with him, seemed a stranger action than could be easily explained. Mabel looked him full in the face, and answered in a low voice,

" I think—she wished to get rid of me. I know she often is talking to him about *something* very earnestly, but whenever I come in she stops. And she imagined you would be reading, and never heed me."

Wat said nothing to that; but he took up the book she had been pretending to pore over. It was only a collection of fairy stories she had picked up from the drawing-room table, but the open page caught his eye.

It was a childish tale of a little Princess Goldenlocks; so called from her wondrous hair. She was oppressed by a harsh step-mother, so wandered out alone into the wide world, with pretty, bare, bleeding feet, trying ever to reach the kingdom of her only relation, who had been the friend of her dead father and mother. And on the way she met with a poor serving-man, uncouth and ill-shapen, and hairy of face, but generous and faithful, with a great and loving heart, who humbly devoted himself to her service, and carried her over all the rough and stony places, and protected her through all dangers, till at last they reached the great king's fair realm. And there the king decreed that she must part with this serving-man, or else (because sweet Goldenlocks wept) she might marry the poor ugly loon, and forget her rank.

So Goldenlocks looked at the city and the palace, and looked at the face of her patient servitor, now dumb and pale, and stepping down, gave him her hand;—whereupon up-rose a great shout from the crowd around, for the serving-man's ill-looks had passed away, and his face shone with sudden beauty; and all men knew him as the lost son of the king.

What made Wat look up at the girl?

Did he appear to her as rude and uncouth as that serving-man? he wondered; for it was foreign to his downright nature to pay the constant slight flatteries and attentions that he believed many young ladies thought indispensable in a gentleman's behaviour—of his age, at least. He had just now prevented this little Miss Langton from running off in a huff, as authoritatively as he would one of his own romping little cousins down in Nor-folk, whom he used alternately to lecture, scold, and make himself a slave unto. She was hardly older, and far less grown. Indeed, custom had so far followed the re-semblance that here he had been reading of "Goldenlocks" without once addressing her.

But it was easy to see that Mabel, curled up again in her corner of the window-seat, was perfectly contented. What did the wild little mistress of Cherrybank know of the manners of young gentlemen, or even of most older ones? Nothing;—less even than many a Sunday-school girl used to seeing gentlefolk. But the instincts of childhood still helped her; and reading Wat's actions by the kindly light of his honest eyes and frank smile, she was satisfied he was her friend, despite Madame; and was a little elated, but wanted no more.

"What were you reading?—ah, 'Goldenlocks.' That is what my sister used to call me. She is a widow now, since two years—Mrs. Lester; and she is coming here soon, only for my sake, because Madame will not allow me to visit her. She is so good and sweet to me—dear Maud!'"

"It will do you good to be with her here, anyway," said Wat, gravely; noticing what a sudden soft lovingness her voice .

took; so different from the harder ring when she spoke of her step-mother. To be under the influence of a sweet and gracious woman would just save her brave, high spirit from being made hard and vindictive at her age, when the mind was plastic, he thought.

"Shall I tell you how it all happened? ... I must! Somehow, during those years after my mother's death, papa did not like that Mrs. Lester should take me from home. I only saw her once a year when she came for about three or four days; though she wrote to me constantly when I was alone. Then he got me a governess; and last Winter he came home himself. Not that we saw him much—he was always studying all night long till near daylight in his own room. But soon the accident happened that has made him so ill. He was half-way up the side of a quarry examining some peculiar formation, when part of the rock beneath him gave way (we suppose it had been loosened by the frost). Of course he got

a terrible fall; was insensible for some time,
and ill for weeks afterwards! . . . . Madame—we arranged I should call her so just
after the marriage, when she was very kind
—Madame took the nursing of him then
entirely—would not let *me* go near him,
saying I disturbed him!"—Mabel's voice
quivered a little. "Then she wrote to
Maud that I required change of air from his
sick-room; so I went willingly; but, before
I came home, she wrote another letter, sign-
ing herself, my devoted *Maman !* Maud was
so angry!"

Wat, though strongly sympathising with
her, yet wished she would not tell him all
this; but he could as soon have stopped
the fountain out there from plashing over
in the evening sunlight. And Mabel herself
hardly yet felt, as would other girls, that it
were better to keep silent concerning the
private affairs of her own family. She was
so young—so inexperienced; to her all
men were strangers simply, or else either

friends or foes.   This man was her friend; and oh! what a relief it was to speak out to him!—to any kind ears!   What should she know of fine, different gradations of acquaintanceship?   As yet, where she gave any trust she gave all; where she gave friendship it was with generous impulse, too fully and freely; but she would learn better, or differently, in the world soon.   Still she had too much pride to tell him anything of her burning anger and disgust when she recalled that marriage of her step-mother; though her lowered voice and unusually quiet utterance betrayed much without her knowing it.

"You are angry with Mrs. Langton for making some mistake about us to-day—and perhaps it is hard on both sides for step-mother and daughter to understand each other.   But be patient; she may grow kinder, and you will be forgiving."

"Neither of us can ever change; it is not in our natures," she cried, in an impassioned tone. "I can love a great deal; but I hate just as strongly. Confess you prefer such feelings to a craven spirit.".

"I think your sentiment a grand one— for paganism."

She felt the rebuke, and was silent: drooping her small head, with its yellow fringe of hair, soft as a mere infant's; but, though really touched, she was not hurt. The few women who knew Wat Huntley well, and loved him dearly, said he could hurt no woman's feelings; and said, too, that, under his plain exterior, there was a charm of manner—a strong attraction to feminine minds—which, in the world at large, might, had he so chosen, have made him, in spite of ugliness, a dangerous rival to other men. Dear old Wat! They would wonder to each other whether any other woman, not one of themselves, would get to know him as they did; but, if so, none doubted she must love him; then and for always. Mabel, too, felt the charm; even her child's heart, like a bud, opened to his warmth of sunny kindliness.

"But tell me more about Mrs. Lester—I like to hear you speaking about her," he went on, drawing nearer, and coaxing her back to joyousness by a topic which seemed so pleasant.

"Oh !—Maud. She is beautiful, and you will like her so much; everybody does. She is dark-haired and tall, with such sweet eyes!"

"Are they the same colour as yours?" he asked, with an idle, happy laugh : but she fancied he was underrating her sister, and flared up.

"Like mine!—red! A wild animal's! You do not deserve to hear another word."

"What have I said now? I never thought yours were red—I don't believe it. Let me see."

She gave a little shrug and a pout, quaint as were many of her gestures; then, leaning on one elbow, turned her head.

"See, if you like;" and slowly, very slowly, as if her full, white eyelids and long lashes were too heavy to raise, she turned her gaze upon him.

Such strange eyes!—brown, tawny-red, gleaming,—one knew not of what colour, so confusing was their fascination—that soft, slow, enchaining, basilisk glance, with a sort of subdued glitter, seeming to lie far below the surface of those swimming depths. An indescribable sensation passed all through Walter, and he drew a long breath, while those eyes looked into his; then she as slowly turned them away, with a slight dawning smile, and he felt almost vexed with himself for acknowledging her power of mesmerism—or was it that alone?

But what to think of her he hardly knew. Was she child or woman?—the mere child he had thought her, through whose eyes another soul had looked one moment with that subtle, all-subduing gleam: —a witch's soul passed already from the too pure tenement? Or a girl with powers she did not fully know, trying them, as now, with a shy, alarmed pride in their possession; as some young savage might exult over deadly but rather incomprehensible fire-arms? The latter, most likely; for she was looking at him with a puzzled, doubtful little air of triumph, since it was not quite the first time she had tried this power, though only upon humble subjects. But now the little mesmerist got a scolding; all the graver that her lecturer felt she had gained a certain power over him.

"That will do," she at last said, stopping her ears. "You talk more than is fair; and I have so much myself to say—to ask you. I want to know, do you feel with me as if our life here was so new and pleasant, —but not *real?* I could almost think you are not *really* here, talking to me; but that you have only stepped out of some book for the moment."

"Could I be the hero?" he asked; and

then gave a curious smile; her face said so plainly he could not.

Why, to her he seemed quite *old!* A faithful, ungainly friend might be his *rôle :* doing good to all, and liked by all; but the hero—that was absurd!

"I own it does seem slightly unusual to have a little lady of your age to talk to; except when I am among my own people," he went on; "and, indeed, as I seldom go into society, I rarely meet older ones."

"But what amusements have you, then, after all your hard work?"

"I stay at home, in barracks," he answered, with a lurking smile on his face; "get through a little reading; have a pipe, by myself or with any other of us who happens to be there; and get hold of a paper."

Mab tried hard for some seconds to picture what charms such a mode of enjoyment could possess, but the premises in her little brain being too vague, she gave up

endeavouring to draw any satisfactory con-
clusions therefrom. So she proceeded to tell
him confidentially of the routine of her old
life (as she called it), which seemed so much
more "real" than this one; till he fancied he
could see her up at daybreak, to see the
sunrise from the common; or at noontide
(when she was "*much* younger"), half-lying
among the sedges of the little Nye, with
her bare feet in the water, and all the
wood rising thick and steep above and
behind her.

When her father's carriage-wheels first
sounded she sprang away eagerly, however,
and he was left alone. But, somehow, the
name of Goldenlocks kept repeating itself
in his brain all the evening—little Goldenlocks!

As for Madame, she returned well-pleased;
having gained her end, in having that certain, most important conversation with her
aged husband, which Mab suspected. She
never even troubled her head as to how her

little ruse had succeeded; if well—why,
good; but if explanations proved necessary,
it would only amuse her to invent them.
She loved these little, and often unneces-
sary, stratagems for their own sake—they
kept her hand in !

CHAPTER V.

"Every white will have its blacke,
And every sweete its soure."

Percy's Reliques.

IT had been raining heavily since morning, and only about four in the afternoon did the weather begin to show signs of clearing, and allow the visitors in the hotel to hope for some fresh air before the *table-d'hôte* dinner at half-past six. Hardly an inmate but felt more bored hour after hour, as the rain came down steadily in great sheets, with a swishing, dreary sound.

Even the occupants of the billiard-room were depressed, despite the help of constant smoking and unintermittent play; and the rolling of the balls sounded at last even monotonous in their ears. They were mostly middle-aged men, with an air of well-shaven prosperity about them; and when, with careful civility, they addressed any stranger, one naturally expected their first remarks (after the weather) to be of shares, or perhaps relative to cotton. But, though well-to-do, such an element could hardly be lively; and only the youngest among them, who considered himself one of the most intelligent and entertaining townsmen in his particular mercantile community, tried to sustain his reputation by painfully laboured little jests and jokes, which at times evoked some heavy laughs or as heavy answering gibes.

Some other groups were composed of more diversified elements, however : there were one or two well-dressed, but little known men, who spoke of London as their dwelling-place with a vagueness which neither they themselves nor any other folk dreamt of changing into a clear definition.

A few officers of the Indian staff-corps,
whose time seemed spent in flirting with
grass-widows, and affording gossip to the
malevolent; and some old country gentlemen,
whose wives were upstairs in private sitting-
rooms, and who had "just looked" in with an
uncomfortable feeling that they ought now
to be cheering the stately solitude of those
better halves. These all—with a small
separate knot of young men of good standing, from whom came some gay remarks
and laughter between the puffs of cigar-
smoke—formed the principal features in the
male section of the varied assemblage.

In the large saloon an equal number of
ladies filled the room, chatting in subdued tones, and frequently eyeing with dis-
favour the occupants of opposition ottomans.
Here, for instance, was a certain "grace"-widow
who had just been singing; but who having
had no admirer to turn the leaves, and receiving chill applause, was revenging herself by
abusing to two simple spinsters the low ma-

lice and envy prevailing among those around. These believed in her as yet with touching credulity; though they had only gathered from her that she was infinitely superior to the "business people" around; that her husband was exiled to some remote region, and that he must, from her accounts, be "a perfect brute !"

In one window-seat sat an old lady, of ample form and benevolent aspect, the double gold chain on whose broad, black-silken bosom heaved and fell with deep-breathed rhythmical regularity as she bent over her "genteel-looking" worsted work. Mrs. Higgins was not given to promiscuous conversation, except with her equals; and these (as she sometimes felt with a slight pang traversing her comfortable defences of flesh and blood, which ought in a measure to have excluded such annoyances) were more rarely to be met with now that Mr. Jacob Higgins had retired from business toils to the repose of such a handsome new house; one with acres of glass, and—she felt certain—far more recent appliances for speaking-tubes, and hot water laid on, than their neighbours. Nevertheless, her large heart was so inclined to kindly condescension that, in spite of having her daughters, Juliana, Mariana, and Christiana Beatrice (besides some sons of various ages, and a pair of romping twin girls), with her to nestle under her wing, she offered her protection to any stray young ladies; assuring them, while smiling broadly, and raising her eyebrows with difficulty up to her well-arranged front, that she was quite equal to all additional responsibility.

"Of course," the grass-widow would whisper, with a little sarcastic laugh, " Since Battle, Murder, and Sudden Death " (as she privately nicknamed the three Misses Higgins), "since they don't trouble the dear soul's mind, no other young ladies would be equal to doing so."

This trio, who, by the way, hated the

speaker with a virtuous disapprobation, as an
interloper in their proper domains, were so
named in reverse order, since the eldest had
increased her eccentricity and love of amusement with years, seeing so few remained, as
she expressed it, "to make hay in." All
three were fine, large young women, with
shining black locks; and just now they were
talking eagerly to an affected young person,
Miss Mawkesworth, who was an orphan and
a reputed great heiress, and whose fuzzy
hair was raised into such a complicated pile
that her head bent always to one side,
languidly unable to support the weight.
Already the widow had nicknamed her the
Golden Pippin, and called her plain middle-
aged companion the Ribston one. She, poor
thing, played duenna; displaying her useful-
ness at times by being judiciously out of the
way.

Naturally the young ladies were dis-
cussing the rival factions in the house, and

by some chance Walter Huntley had fallen under their scalpel.

"Well, Captain Huntley is far from an Adonis, at all events!" one decided, with a nod of contemptuous vigour.

"Now, that is you, Christiana, all the world over!" cried Mariana, who, being older, had naturally learnt to take a more tolerating view of masculine faces and figures. "As if a man's looks mattered a straw in the long run. Not that I admire this one very particularly myself. All I say against him is, that he must be stupid! Fancy a man being in such a crack regiment as the Blacks (some of whom are as great flirts as there are under the sun!), and yet never caring to say a word to one of us. It must be conceitedness, though, for he can be nice."

"I knew them when they were quartered at Brighton," put in the heiress, with a conscious simper and an affected giggle. "As

you say, dear, they were all very sad in that
way—quite naughty."

Juliana had said nothing hitherto, con-
tenting herself with whistling under her
breath, and inciting her Skye terrier into
worrying fiercely the toes of her strong
masculine shoes; now, however, dramatic
instinct told her it was time to strike in with
that vigorous sentiment and strong manly
voice which generally ended such arguments.

" You young women all think yourselves
very wise, no doubt; but I'll have my say,
too ; and the man may be as ugly as sin, but
he is a perfect gentleman, though none of
you may like him. You can leave him to
me; we get on very fairly together."

This was hardly flattering to the rest, and
after a moment's pause or so, none caring to
enter the lists against their redoubted elder,
they changed the conversation.

"Did anyone see who came by yesterday's
afternoon train ?" inquired Miss Mawkes-

worth. "Really I was so shy, I could not look for new names in the visitors' book, with all those gentlemen standing in the hall."

" Not one man arrived, my dear, so *you* won't be interested," Christiana answered, with a cavernous yawn. " Polly and I scampered, as usual, to see the bus arriving; but there were only a tall footman and a French maid belonging to a grand old widow —a Mrs. Cust. Why, what were you after not to be there? You are generally as much on the look-out as any of us?"

"He, he! How you wild girls do rattle on, and quiz poor little me, to be sure. I— I was only taking a walk, to drink my strong iron," simpered the young lady, as she drooped her head with shy embarrassment more sideways than ever.

" Oh! no apologies, my sweet innocent— *we* know better," answered that terrible Juliana. (The truth was, the Golden One had been straying off artlessly with young

Mr. Higgins. Not the eldest—he was intended to contract an alliance in high aristocratic circles, or even to content himself among the older landed gentry—but the second son, an ingenuous youth, with 'sprouting yellow whiskers, and of a somewhat pimpled countenance. (He might be encouraged to "marry money" with advantage to the Higgins family).

The rain was stopping now; and in that dun canopy overhead there was clearly a great rift, which widened and widened till, all of a sudden, yellow beams of cheering, rousing sunlight slanted downwards on the grass before the windows, and that bright streak broadened, while between the trees one saw the great masses of blue-black rain clouds rolling away towards Knaresborough. In a few minutes the sun was gleaming on the fresh-washed trees and leaves and grass-blades in the garden; playing on the fountain; sparkling on minute particles of the fine sandy gravel on the walks; tenderly warming the broken, earth-stained pinks and verbenas; giving a new life and interest to everything, even to the sight of the gutters, down which runnels of whitish-brown water were rapidly twisting and flowing, contemplated with strutting, impudent philosophy by some wag-tails, who balanced those latter appendages with even more conscious pride than usual.

Mrs. Higgins was looking out of the window with such an interested, following gaze that her daughters at last became aware of the fact, and, in their anxiety to see anything that might be new, all exclaimed, "Law, ma, what is it?" and, rushing to stare out over her head, nearly reduced the poor, fat old soul to a large modern mummy.

Only Captain Huntley walking up and down by the sunniest wall, giving his arm to an old bent, white-haired man! As if that were worth coming to see! Mrs. Higgins's half stifled rejoinder, that she considered it quite a "beautiful sight," and that—besides

his old family (in the next shire to theirs)
she was sure the young man had a good 'art,"
—was contemptuously hooted by Mariana.

"Good fiddlestick! He's *worthy*—that's
what he is; and of worthy young men I
always wash my hands." (What a thanksgiving Huntley would have uttered, had he
been aware of that mental act of ablution !)

"That is old Mr. Langton—a poor, silly
Methusaleh," said Crissy. "Captain Huntley is always talking to that shy little
daughter of his, who is dressed such a scare-
crow."

"That little chit! Oh, nonsense, my
dear! Why, she is a mere child," objected
Miss Mawkesworth, raising her usually
whispering voice slightly more sharply, and
lifting her chin from Crissy's shoulder, where
it had been affectionately resting, while,
with her arm through that young woman's,
she, too, looked out.

It began to dawn in Miss Mawkesworth's
dull mind that these Higgins girls were

very upsetting in assuming that they alone could bring about the future subjugation of this gentleman, whom they evidently considered a "somebody." Oh, they might think her a fool, but she was not to be so easily blinded.   To be put off, indeed, with young Josh Higgins, while they monopolised the society of this live Captain in the Blacks! But she could see through their designs, for all they pretended to be so honest and boisterous—a pretence which did not take her in.   She was cleverer than they thought.   So, while she put down her chin more affectionately than before on her friend's shoulder, and rubbed her chignon against the other's black plaits, it was with the dull, cunning resolve of a fool, that it would be a very good thing to give a lesson to these noisy girls, and to show them that such a fortune as hers was more likely to command respect than they imagined.   As I said, she observed that Mabel was only a chit, and most reprehensibly inclined to give herself high and mighty airs, as if she were one bit better than other people.

"Ah, yes, to be sure; I daresay," said old Mrs. Higgins, picking up her dangling worsted with its needle again. "That very ladylike, sweet person, her stepmother, was telling me only yesterday what a trial she was to herself and the poor old father—and how anxious she was to do her duty by the girl. A most right-minded young woman is Mrs. Langton, but I fear has a hard time before her, so attached as she is to her poor, dear 'usband, and with his daughter's ill-tempered disposition——"

"Oh, stop, mother; do! I vow and declare it drives me wild to hear you!" suddenly burst out Juliana, with a force and reality which showed she was thoroughly in earnest; adding more gently, as she saw a hurt and rather alarmed feeling actually succeeding in spreading its expression over her mother's face (in which the eyes seemed struggling not to be entirely obliterated, reminding one—with a resemblance which, despite respect for her good-heartedness, would assert itself—of a large, amiable, white Yorkshire pig). "You are an old dear; you know you are!—but as to people's characters, any baby that had just got its first tooth would be as wise; and what you would do without me to look after you, I don't know. Now I like the Langton child. She is a proud, shy, little spitfire, but of a good sort. I said to her yesterday, 'Here, child, just go and fetch me that book from the end of the room,' and the little puss calmly called up one of the waiters who was passing, and desired him to give it to me, with the air of a duchess. Quite right of her, too, to hold her own; but that foreign woman gives me the creeps —a cold, venomous snake!"

Good Mrs. Higgins had only succeeded in giving utterance, just after the originally startling sentence, to one slow, thick-voiced " Ju-ly !" and now contentedly resumed the shading of her full-blown roses of correctly opposite hues, but painfully similar blue-green leaves. She was aware of a dim perception within her, which had not yet struggled into an idea, that somehow girls were altogether different from what she remembered in her young days; but yet, again, Juliana could hardly be wrong, since she was so much cleverer than her old mother. And Mr. Higgins had always made so much of his July, who took after himself, that perhaps her forwardness, even in short frocks, was not to be wondered at.

CHAPTER VI.

"Sweet loving-kindness! if thou shine,
The plainest face may seem divine,
And beauty's self grow doubly bright
In the mild glory of thy light."

DR. MACKAY.

MABEL LANGTON was coming shyly out into the garden; and her father, seeing her, stopped his slow walk to lean on Huntley's arm. As she drew nearer he even eyed her with an unusual expression of interest. He was looking at the timid little face (which had suddenly brightened so wondrously) with a curious expression: partly a faint fatherly pride, which had been all his life hitherto almost utterly stifled; partly the searching gaze of that timid, suspicious nature which had so shut him out from his kin.

Did no instinct tell him that she was blushing with frightened pleasure at that faint sign of the awaking interest she fancied,—yet almost feared to hope,—he had occasionally felt for her during the last few days? Signs which she had so longed for all her lonely short life, with the pining of a soul starving for want of love—hoping dumbly, yet vainly, through her loneliness all those weary years; reverencing his learning that to her seemed so vast; proud of any echo of fame that reached her seclusion.

And she would have given him back so passionate a response from a heart which could not expend all its treasures of warm affection on her four-footed pets and companions; on the dear old inanimate objects around; or even on those kind-hearted dependants and friends to her in childhood, who had so often pitied the "poor little maid," and wondered her father should never once throw her a kind word—not so much as even a look.

"Why, my little girl is quite growing up into a young lady!" the old man said, turning his head towards Walter with a half-smile. "Will you care to walk up and down here with us, Mabel?—though our talk will have small interest for you. My daughter is, perhaps, not much educated, Captain Huntley; but my theory is that health, and the power of enjoying life, are in themselves an education. The sciences are not playthings, to be toyed with as some women idly do; and more exhaustive studies only wear and fret their physical powers, unfitting them for the one special part assigned them alone in the great plan of creation. But to me, sir, it is a pleasure —a satisfaction—to find a comparatively young man like you electing to converse with an old one—a young man, too, who has used his eyes to advantage. I have spoken with some at times who boasted what remote districts of Asia and other places they had visited . . . yet could not even describe the appearance of the country they had seen, much less the formations of rocks— could relate nothing of the soils or minerals, flora or fauna,—knowing only what animals they had shot in their love of sport, which therefore alone yielded profit."

Miles Langton spoke slowly, as if laboriously deciphering words in a mental book, and with frequent pauses, sometimes from want of cohesion in ideas. Though still, when excited by discussions upon his favourite themes, he could somewhat rouse his dying powers, and force them to obey him for the moment. He was nervously aware himself of these sad symptoms, but endeavoured painfully to hide his growing weakness from others.

"I fear I can take no credit to myself for using my brains to very much purpose," said Wat, whom praise from this far more profoundly read old man humbled. "Even as a small schoolboy, in a very short jacket, I always liked collecting different stones, and hunting for rare birds' nests; so perhaps the habit of staring about stuck to me afterwards. But I am only a rough soldier, and know next to nothing, as you do, of really deep studies, or sound and thoroughly scientific reasonings; and only judge for myself, as best I can, by what my own eyes have seen, and what little learning one picks up."

"Ah yes—empirical, empirical," muttered old Miles, who only seemed to grasp part of what the other said. "But, sir, we must crawl before we stand upright, creep before we walk, and imbibe strong draughts of the knowledge which those before us— before us—have stored, if we would dare to wrestle with others on the vast plains of Science. And some who have worked and toiled hard—ay, day and night,—will find themselves foiled—baffled, by—themselves ! Nature, struggling against the mind, and, it may be, struggling for its own base corporeal existence. Who can cope against such internal treachery; when failing powers, dazzled sight, swimming brain—all!—all!—refuse to exert themselves?—to rouse themselves up from that blackness which falls, like a thick, vaporous pall, just as the procession is passing of those great Thoughts, Causes, TRUTHS, which you have waited your life long to see. Then, . . . in the darkness, . . . they are sweeping by; touching you softly with their garments as they pass—but you cannot seize them—cannot grasp and hold them fast!"

He had stopped in his slow walk as the thoughts grew upon him, for once clear and connected: stopped, leaning forward on Huntley's arm, with a painfully-fixed, far-away gaze; but still his voice grew stronger and more unbroken, and his right hand pointed slightly forwards. Then at the last words his vision seemed to return nearer and earthward. His hand dropped, and his voice died away into a low, weak regret,—the deep pathos of an unsatisfied, failing, yet still earth-clinging soul.

Just then a lady came out into the sunshine by the side-door. It was Mrs. Langton, as Walter recognised by the Frenchwoman's easy grace of habit with which she raised her dress and picked her way along the gravel, showing her long, narrow feet; with a something feline about her also, as, cat-like, she seemed to fawn even in the distance, while carefully avoiding every speck of wet or dirt in her noiseless advance.

" Ah, *mon ami*, you are exciting yourself. I have come to persuade you in,—Mabelle!" (and as she turned to say something in a cold, measured undertone to the young girl, old Miles Langton's face changed into its usual vague, listless expression; but Mabel's hardened, and she abruptly left them). "Captain Huntley, will you still give my husband your arm to our sitting-room? Ah, so; thank

you. It is really too good and kind!" So
saying, she bestowed a sweet smile upon
Wat's ugly, unimpressible visage; but she
might as well have smiled at a horse-
block.

"Is not the child coming in too?" asked
poor Miles, gazing round. Walter looked
round quickly too—it might have been to
see which way Mabel took.

"No, no," soothingly answered his wife,
"you would not have her lose her health
indoors always? Ah! here we are—and
you, will not you come in also, M. le Capi-
taine; it will be a pleasure?"

But Wat had his letters by the evening
post to read over a cigar. He was very
sorry, but was afraid . . . a cold parting
smile, and the door closed suddenly on his
half-finished sentence, and on Madame's pale
face; whereat our friend gave an astonished,
broad grin.

"Will you walk into my parlour, said the
spider to the fly," he quoted under his

breath, still staring at the door; and then
with a relieved air betook himself down the
dim passage.

"Mad! stark, staring mad!" decided
Mariana, *sotto voce;* who was slily peeping
down the well-stairs from a flight above.
"Grimacing and muttering to himself in that
way!" and she laid up that amongst other
valuable bits of information she had collected respecting Captain Walter Huntley and
his idiosyncrasies.

Half an hour later, and we may find him
again, walking up and down a gravelled
path which led towards the fields. He was
finishing both his cigar and a letter from
his aunt in Norfolk, asking him to come and
see them when he left Harrogate, and re-
proaching him for waiting till his leave in England was almost over, without having paid
them another visit. The letter was interesting in its way, so why need he look every
now and then over the grass plot to a bench
under a witch-elm, where one small, solitary

figure was seated, wearing even at that distance a look of forlorn disconsolateness?

Poor little thing! How dejected she
seemed! He might just as well have stroll-
ed up and down there. Why he turned off
here at the last moment, he hardly knew.
What nonsense imagining, however, that
anything he could say would amuse her!
He smiled at his own conceitedness, and yet
—what a plague she would think him!—but
he must go and speak to her, and find out
whether anything had gone wrong.

Mabel did feel lonely; nay more, she told
herself she felt wretched,—miserable! Why
was everything so contrary in even the
smallest events of her life? Why was she,
who could so love everyone, always condemned to repulse from those around,—who
so thoroughly enjoyed life, to have each
hour made burdensome by constant, cun-
ningly petty annoyances? She had been
simple enough, poor child, to be fond of
Madame at first, who had been kind to her

until her marriage, as the cobra capella might seem when fascinating its victims into helplessness, before enveloping them in its stifling folds.

If only that woman had never come to Cherrybank! The accident to her father might have happened all the same; but then she, Mabel, would alone have nursed him, and brought him here. No hateful stranger would have interfered, as did this one to-day, between herself and him.

" How are you getting on, Miss Langton? I fancied you hardly seemed happy over here. Perhaps you are chilled; that bench is too damp for you to be sitting on." So said Walter, speaking carelessly, as he halted beside her on his stroll, since he perhaps wished to impress upon himself that he had only come round there by chance, without any really distinct purpose. (There had not been more than fifty yards to be traversed before he had come up to her; yet it was possible to have gone through several different but dove-tailing phases of mind since then.)

Mabel looked up with a start. What made him come there; as if he or anyone else cared a straw whether she were happy, or eating her heart out with useless repinings? If her own father,—if her own kith and kin,—starved her by withholding all sympathy, she would be too proud to accept any crusts from strangers.

"I am not particularly unhappy at all, thank you. But I came here because I wished to get away from *everybody*, and be left in peace," she answered, turning her head with pride and temper.

"I have been disturbing you, then? I beg your pardon, I must try not to commit such a blunder again."

"Well—one is not always inclined to talk to strangers."

Courteously—but at once—he left her.

Miss Mabel, however, looked after him with both eyebrows met in a frown; biting her lips, yet with a suspicion of tears in her dark, red-brown eyes. He was gone; and she closed her hands tightly in self-anger, because she always was so rude to the few people who did show her kindness, while looking in vain towards others. And Captain Huntley had been such a friend to her these last few days.

So, being even more miserable than before, she hunched herself up and glowered, clasping her knees, for she could not help acting every second of her life—only her acting was the outcome of her own feelings, not the assumed expression of those of others.

(A smart head with a jaunty cap was peeping carefully out past the dimity curtains in one of the servants' third-story attics; and the head nodded, put itself knowingly on one side, and then nodded again, as if it, too, knew all about it).

Meanwhile, Huntley was taking a long, tiresome walk into the country, telling himself it was the wet day that had put him

out of temper, and made bracing exercise
necessary. He told himself, too, he was a
fool for taking too great interest in other
folk's private affairs, and having to be set
straight by a mere little school-girl; yet he
had grown to be on such warm and friendly
terms with the child, surely she need not
have repelled him, as she would everybody.
It had only been charitable to give the poor
old man an arm this afternoon; but he
should certainly not annoy the daughter
again by forcing his society upon her.

Yet he had felt strong partiality for her,
even in her ill-temper!—as one forgives and
cares for a child again, whether it will or not.
And perhaps the poor little thing had been
really unhappy, and was therefore irritable.
He guessed that step-mother of hers made
her frequently so ; and how well they had
got on together down at Birk Crag ! No ;
still—he could not *quite* forgive her for
repulsing his sympathy, and hurting his
warm, honest feelings so unaccountably ;

though, at the same time, it mattered nothing at all to him—nothing. All the same, he walked farther and farther, coming back muddy and hot and tired; late for dinner, and out of gear with Harrogate (a tiresome, rainy hole) and things in general. As to the child, he had then forgiven her. He had insensibly been thinking too much that his friendship was a help to her —that was all.

That night, about eleven o'clock, if we peeped in at the attic window before mentioned (since the shutters are not closed, and there is a space between the curtains), we might see Miss Hitchcocks seated at the table, busily writing in her " diry" by the light of a solitary mould candle. The last entry is short, but—though she contemplates the writing with satisfaction, with her head on one side—she nibbles her pencil, as if in doubtfulness about the subject-matter, pursing her lips with an air as if things in general were tangled, and the pattern of affairs lately

ᛌ hard to cut out.   The entry runs as follows :

"Much, I fear me, my young missis ᛌand the Capting has fell out, and I as thought my Bewty had met her Beest! I didn't think to hencourage it at first, till Mr. Brown told me he and the principle waiters all approves of him as a *real* gentleman, but wish, all the same, he would turn into Prince Charmin'—the sooner the better, as far as happerences goes. New missis more cutting an' cantankyrous than ever, as I was a-brushing her ᛌ'air. Poor, poor Agnes Hitchcocks!—What it is to be a maid!"

CHAPTER VII.

"Tell me where is Fancy bred,
    Or in the heart or in the head?
How begot, how nourishéd?
        —Reply, reply.

It is engender'd in the eyes,
    With gazing fed; and Fancy dies
In the cradle where it lies."

SHAKESPEARE.

THERE were raised eyebrows next morning in the concert-room of the Royal chalybeate spa; for some of our acquaintances in the hotel saw their grass-widow, Mrs. Smith, entering demurely, in the company of a slight, not full-grown, but high-bred-looking girl, to whom she was affording her somewhat slender protection, while her usual close cavalier was not in attendance.

The truth was, these two harmless yet maligned individuals had had a slight misunderstanding, and were now consequently more dubious as to the affinity which had hitherto seemed to exist so harmoniously between their kindred souls. Therefore, since it would gratify her enemies were she to be seen totally deserted, the widow had begged Mrs. Langton to allow Mabel to go with her—to which that lady, for reasons of her own (the principal one being that her old husband had timidly asked that Mab might walk with him instead of herself), had consented.

Not knowing this, however, several eyes looked in surprise over the tumblers out of which their owner were drinking iron waters through glass tubes. Our friend Wat Huntley wondered, for one; but then he remembered it was really none of his business—though it was a shame to put the child under such care : worse, in his opinion, than suffering her to go alone. So he

took his way down the glass-roofed room,
going out into the garden beyond, where a
band was playing, the sun shining, and a
fresh wind blowing through the tree-tops.

Mabel saw him turn away, and her heart
swelled a little; poor little girl! She had
repented so bitterly of her great rudeness
yesterday, and had meant to tell him so
when, as usual, he came beside her at
dinner: but his empty chair was hardly a
good proxy for such a confession. All the
time the meal lasted, while her father sat
bent and silent, and Madame was captivating her neighbours, she had been troubling
her puzzled head about him. Was he ill?—
was he only dining later?—was he angry?
She *hoped* he was, she was so vexed herself.

But another phase came when, dinner
being over, Madame, as usual, marshalled
her victims to their sitting-room, whence all
sweet Summer twilight was excluded, and
the gas-burners only made gaudy fire-papers
and stiff furniture look less home-like than

ever. Next, Mrs. Langton had languidly disposed herself, in an elegant attitude, on the sofa, with a yellow-covered French novel, which she studied (smiling disagreeably to herself), or dozed over. Her husband, meanwhile, had been already established by her in the solitary arm-chair, and desired, with gentle firmness, to go to sleep—an order which, as she had thrown a handkerchief over his meek head, and as he never moved, it was to be presumed her weary old Tithonus had obeyed.

Mabel alone sat bolt upright, under the gaslight, studying a history of the great French Revolution, and occasionally writing down, with painstaking minuteness, dates of almost every day in Brumaire, or Floréal, or Thermidor. For Madame's commands were, "not to lean back—to imbue her mind well with these events; and to revere that as a glorious age, whose heroes were to be adored, and their deeds exulted over!"

More than ever our little heroine had

hated the accounts of their blood-imbrued
orgies, and sickening scaffold-dances and
devilries, since she longed to hear the tea-
gong sound, and have another chance of
looking round for that friendly, ugly face
which hitherto always turned ·to her—no
matter at how great a distance—with a
kindly smile, as the unbeauteous sunflower
turns to the sun.   How her feet had danced
with impatience as she had slowly followed
her father leaning on Madame, in to tea at
last.   Then, taking her place, raised. her
eyes—but Huntley was seated beside Miss
Higgins, laughing and talking with her,
never seeing his penitent little friend !

After tea it was nine o'clock, so Madame
soon despatched her invalid to bed ; to
which, as to all her dictates, he meekly
submitted.   Poor Mabel being set to a half
hour's edifying study of classical mythology;
unrelieved by any beautifying explanations
of how these hoary myths were born long
ago, when the world was fresh and young.

That over, it was a relief to receive the cold dismissal to her bed-room, where she sat proudly mute and unhappy while Agnes brushed her hair; doing her best, kind soul, to make the process as soothing as possible.

Then, when alone in the darkness, she repeated over and over again her words to Huntley; now excusing, now even heightening their tone of petulant rudeness. Nothing could soothe her ashamed and penitent self-reproach, when she recalled his constant kindness but his vexed expression that day, till she had sternly resolved to make an abject apology the very first thing next morning; which settled, conscience allowed her, after tossing for what seemed hours (it was about half a one), to go to sleep.

But now matters seemed far from as easy as she had imagined; perhaps Mrs. Smith might not go into the garden. Why! Where *was* she? And Mabel looked round in the crowd like a lost child; then, perceiving the widow just departing jauntily by

a side-door, in company with a fresh, masculine, familiar friend, her forgotten charge
scurried after her like a frightened rabbit.
Emerging into the garden, she only found
that both had disappeared down some shady
path, and were either perfectly oblivious of
her existence, or not particularly anxious for
her company.   Perhaps for the first time in
her life poor Mabel suffered from being in a
false position; from feeling herself the only
girl there, among all those strangers, without
any care-taker.   Till lately, in fearless self-
reliance, she had been wont to look out at
all the world from under her firm, straight,
young brows with proud, though wary courage.   Now, despite an effort at braveness,
unbidden tears stole into her eyes as she
stopped irresolutely where two walks met.
Wat's heart felt touched with pity for her
look of desertion and loneliness, as, coming
towards her, he recognised the little figure,
her dress blown tightly by the wind, and the
light shining on her black glazed sailor hat,

standing alone in full relief, and looking wistfully away before her.

She heard the step however: turning her head in something of the fashion of a bird, glancing round in bright wariness without moving its body.

"Here he is!—Oh! what *is* to be done, now?" she said to herself, half crying, half laughing at the absurdity of her nervousness, and because she had forgotten every word she had settled to say.

"Now, Mabel! Mabel! *don't* be a coward! What is there to be frightened at?" (If only he had not been so good to her father —her old father, whose white head was sacred in her eyes—she might have been twice as rude without minding.) "Now!— now!"

Thus little Miss Langton tried to screw her courage to the sticking-point, with compressed lips, and guilty pink spots on her cheeks, as Walter approached, who, half-prepared to—but did not just yet raise his hat.

For it is to be feared he thought.to himself, in sudden cowardice, "What is coming? She is offended again! Walter Huntley, stand your ground. If ever you were in for a terrible scolding, my dear boy, you are now!"

"Captain Huntley, I want to speak to you."

"With pleasure, Miss Langton—good morning, by the way," answered our hero, whose valour felt by no means proof against the wrath of his pet tigress-kitten, and who basely hoped in Providence that abject humility and a nervous smile might disarm her. She stamped her foot.

"Never mind good mornings!" ("Oh, it's all up now—no mistake about it!") "What I want to say is, that I was rude yesterday, but I did not mean it——Stay, that's a fib! I *did* mean it; but I—I don't now."

To save her life she would not have said she was sorry; and even now this humbling of her pride had quite broken down her firmness; added to last night's torments lest her first friend—her kind, only friend— should never forgive her. Her lips, red as two halves of a cherry, quivered,—then drooped pitiably at the corners, instead of being firmly compressed into proper dignity.

"You good little—I mean, my dear Miss Langton,—I did not mind it one bit, I assure you : not in the least. Stop—stop! Wait a moment, and don't go off like that. Listen! I did mind it. I was ferocious, and took a long walk—was late for dinner! There, now, I am glad you will listen reasonably. Shake hands."

It was almost as much a dispensation of Providence, as what many people term such, that Mrs. Smith was nowhere near; for she would certainly have said it was odd to have seen Huntley, of all men in the world, in such warm conversation with any young lady. Nor might he have held that small hand just as long, or in such a friendly way, (to himself it seemed a caressing, protecting gesture, as of a sedate older monitor); smiling down at her with so well-pleased an expression that she looked up with glad restored confidence: a re-established happy gleam in her eyes, and a silent laugh on her whole face. Then, her expression suddenly changing, she drew her hand rapidly away, and turned her head.

"Sit down here, and talk to me for a few minutes, won't you?"

That very morning he would have said such a proceeding, without her care-takers, was not fitting for the child; now he was only anxious to have her all to himself for a few moments.

"Do you know that I felt terribly snubbed yesterday? You sent me straight off—would not even speak to me," he rambled on, in his now beatific state of mind, as she silently seated herself. "But you will talk to me this afternoon instead— eh?"

"If *she* allows me. I was punished for being with you and papa yesterday," answered Mabel, with resigned bitterness.

"Why, she is not really ever harsh to you, is she? Tell me. I can't imagine how she well could."

His voice had grown quite tender, as to a pitied child, while he spoke, his arm resting conveniently on the back of the bench. But Mabel was far from aware of his protecting expression, or that he was looking fondly at her sunshiny plaits and the tip of one small ear, delicate as a curious ivory carving. She was gazing forward —away into dreamy vacancy.

"No, she is not exactly cruel; she dare not be so, I think, while——"

"While what? Tell *me*—won't you?"

"While papa lives!" There was a dread in her low voice, which was mostly for the weak and failing old man, yet partly a cold shadow thrown from her own future. "You can see for yourself he does not care for

her; only he is so feeble. But I think—
oh! Captain Huntley, don't you think too?
—that he *does like me a little !*"

That burst out from her soul like a long-
repressed cry. She did so want some one
—anyone—to strengthen her in her self-
delusion; yet all the while she knew it was
a delusion.

Which, perhaps, of our older selves—women especially,—dare acknowledge any the
more that some trouble which always makes
its home at our hearths, is so unalterable?
Do we not rather try to persuade our sickening hearts that its features are really hope-
ful, growing brighter?—endeavouring to
eat, drink, and be merry, while carefully
averting our gaze from that cold presence.

Walter tried his best to utter what consoling assurances he could; but he had, unfortunately, already made up his mind that
Mr. Langton no more cared for this bright-
haired, dowdy young daughter of his whom
he neglected, than would a bookworm,

gnawing its mouldy way to light, for a
spotted ladybird. And it was so difficult to
him not to be honest that his voice had
hardly the true ring of convinced sincerity.

Mab knew it, and bit her under-lip
viciously with her sharp, white teeth.
What a weak thing she was to ask him!
He was only giving her sympathy, not
comfort; she should have kept her sorrow
sacred. So she only nodded her head,
while he invented vague histories (delivered
as airily, and with as great an appearance
of reality as possible) about all the cold-
seeming parents he had known, whose
secret affection for their children was as
rigidly concealed from outer gaze as the
Spartan boy's stolen fox. These coming
abruptly to a conclusion, both were silent.
Mabel glued her lips together, drawing
patterns on the gravel; but Walter felt quite
unhappy for her. "Tender-hearted little
soul that she was!—and such a brave girl
too!" He was longing to *do* something for

her : but what could he do ? Had she been but *much* younger, to be petted and told not to vex herself with crying for the moon ! He wished she had been so, for then he could have taken this forlorn Goldenlocks into his arms just now, so near as she was— almost touching him,—and have made her smile again up in his eyes with that queer, strange look in hers that still haunted him, —the look of some wild deer—and then—

"A penny for your thoughts, Captain Huntley."

Wat started, and blushed—yes, actually blushed; though it was hard to perceive it on that sunburnt face.

"What want of thought to startle a poor invalid like that ! I hope you are sorry, for I feel quite ill," he said, with a very conscious laugh, mimicking nervousness to hide some real embarrassment, while she laughed too with childish malice.

"I am not one bit sorry ! Do you know Madame told me one day that I had the black soul of a young murderess;—but I was not greatly surprised! She holds up my sins to me so often that to save trouble I generally think of myself as a piece of living iniquity."

"Well—I have not yet found out that you are exactly inkily sinful; but what was this unfortunate little tiff about?"

"She ordered my old dog to be drowned in our Nye, and I raved at her. He was cross and blind, certainly; but I like poor creatures that no one else will care for; and they love you so much more in return." (Walter wondered in his heart whether that were the principle upon which she had taken a fancy to him? He was so little well-favoured that most likely it was; and he smiled to himself, thinking of the end of her sentence.) Presently she said, with shy humbleness,

"Is it *true* that I am very rude and un-mannered, compared with other girls? I don't much mind Madame's calling me a learned young she-bear; but I do feel I have not been brought up like most people's daughters. I have only you to ask—what do you· think of me?"

What could he say? She was as pleasant in his eyes as flowers in May; but then she was only a child-bud, or little more. That precisely had placed them in their respective positions, though perhaps it was the dawnings of a woman's wider thoughts and more graciously unselfish ways—the struggle, when the maiden's tender dignity would momentarily assert itself, to lapse again into the old free carelessness which had so enthralled his fancy. For his own part he could not wish her different; yet—as she must grow older some day—he ought perhaps to give her the best advice he could, and so he told her.

"And life in the world will be a different thing from what you have known so far," he said, trying to repress indulgence, and speak like a didactic elder brother. "You can't go through it playing in the sunshine half the day, and being sulky with Mrs. Langton the other half. Only try to be gentle and gracious, and more forgiving; and when you become better used to society, you will turn out as well as any accomplished young lady yet." (A hundred times truer and fresher, he thought to himself; but had the wisdom not to say so.)

"I have not a single accomplishment; that is true," she answered, sighing a little. "Maud came to stay with me once, when her husband died; and all the ladies around who called were so shocked at my ignorance. What stupid women they were too —only talking miserable small gossip, that I hated! But poor Maud was frightened lest what my old schoolmaster had taught would make me an oddity, so she implored papa to let her give me masters. He disliked interference unhappily, so she went home at once, and he himself engaged Madame without any inquiries. One woman-smatterer was as good as another, he said.

"But what did you do in the years before she came?"

"Well, after poor mamma died, you see, I was quite lonely. For a long time he was away, while I ran about, wild. He gave me my pony, and a groom for myself, and made me learn calisthenics once a week—for he said the old Greeks knew the value of exercise for the health, and without perfect health they could never have attained their type of beauty." (Wat remembered how the old man had lately insisted to him on a similar argument, averring that health and beauty went hand-in-hand, and that the culture of both made the mind alive to all beautiful externals, whether of nature or art, instead of turning to morbid inward contemplation. How strange the contrast between his theory for his child and his own subjective, brooding spirit!) "So, in the early mornings, Summer and Winter, I had glorious rides, scouring the country through our lanes.

No doubt, if we knew our neighbours, papa would wish me to play ball with their daughters, like white-armed Nausicaa among her maidens; but none come through our gates now—only on Sundays I peep at a few over our old horse-box of a pew. In the evenings my old master came, and that was my one great pleasure. He was cross and surly often, but not much with me, and he made me read—grand old books, that made one *think;* and how he railed at me when, he said, my thoughts were the brainless products of my sex's thoughtlessness for generations! Those dear old bygone times!"

Her eyes brightened, and were luminous now; her whole face seemed ennobled into a higher order of being—reverential, enthusiastic, passionately, if dimly, worshipping some embodiment of the intellectual.

"And your books—what were they? Tell me more."

"Oh, anything and everything, almost; but we best liked tracing out old religions and dead philosophies; reading about Gnosticism, or of fire and tree worshippers, and old-world histories; arguing over Stoics or Epicureans—and I—why are you laughing? —I defended the Stoa."

Oh! Zeno—ancient Zeno!—surely the blood in even your torpid veins would have stirred, your old heart roused to pleasant mirth, at thoughts of such a sunny-haired disciple : a young, round-limbed thing, striving to walk sedately, without freak or gambol, in such arid ways, bare of all sweet natural instincts—scornful of pain, and submitting all the warm upleapings of nature to the chill tests of philosophy and experience.

" Well, in the Winter evenings I used to bury myself in my books by the fire, and prepare for next day; but if it was Summer, I slipped out in the moonlight, down our dell, then over the river and up through the woods. Sometimes I went higher, to where our neighbour's deer-park marches with our wood, and climbed the wall by a way I knew. Do you know how lovely it is to come out from the darkness and rustling leaves, and see great, dim lawns lying down below you in the hollow, with the bracken on the hill-side all tipped with silver in the strange, soft light, while the deer come bounding gently past in long leaps, like beautiful living shadows?"

Walter looked at her with a sort of surprised gladness, for she had touched a chord to which his inner nature had always passionately responded. Nature-worship was to him almost a sacred creed, though a secret one; for brought up, as he was, among our English people, who starve all such feelings by seeming ashamed of their everyday expression, as a tree stripped of its leaves fails for want of outer aliment, he had learnt to hide the intense sensibility to beautiful impressions upon which many of his acquaintance might have bantered him.

"Know? Yes, that I do!" he answered

in emphatic earnest. "Ours is a glorious old world, after all ; even still it is very good."

This was a new bond of sympathy, which pleased both, mutually surprised they had only now found out its existence. But after a time they came back to the great education question.

"I do so despise the miserable little things Madame teaches me," said Mab, with a small sigh. "To make anti-macassars and paper flowers; and to learn the dry, dry dates of the French Revolution ! And, oh ! Captain Huntley, I did so long to know something of Geology, because"—and she went on with downcast eyes—"it is papa's great study, and I thought, perhaps, if I could please him some day by showing him I knew a little of it, and could enter into his pursuits, why—we might be so happy together." (A most unlikely accomplishment of hopes, alas ! poor, fond little dreamer).

"Why not try, at all events," said Wat

cheerily; " I shall be sending up to town for some books " (he had never thought of it before), " and I should be delighted to give you some I have no further use for ; while you are welcome to any poor help my brains can afford you."

Mabel's gleeful gratitude did his very heart good. The whole way back to the house she expatiated upon the acquisitions of learning she would store up, the specimens she would hoard.

" I have just two, so far ; a bit of Cupid's Meshes—you know that ?"

" Not at all," said Walter, promptly suppressing a little smile as he watched a stray tress of curling hair.

" Not ? Why, rock-crystal, with red oxide of titanium crossing it. And my amethyst crystals. Once I told our old gardener they would save him from being drunk, and he at once begged for the loan of them. But," she went on, changing her lively childish tone for one of sober pleading, " would it be too great trouble—would you *much* mind telling me privately in future, when I have seemed rude or disagreeable? Though it was unpleasant, I always did feel the better afterwards when my old master stormed at my carelessness; though, of course, I hate heartily whoever corrects me."

"You do? Then many thanks for offering me the situation. It is about the pleasantest one I have heard of for some time."

"Don't be afraid; I like him *now!* But Maud is too gentle to find any fault with me when we do meet; while my father—it would be selfish to wish he should turn his mind from great subjects to such an insignificant one; and I do not mind Madame's continual railings."

"But supposing you don't mind me much more?"

"Ah! but I might—occasionally, for I sometimes agree in your opinions, so there is more chance of believing you in the right." Sometimes agree! Bless the child; in her heart it was ever and always, though some new woman's feeling caused that to be hidden from his knowledge.

"Then we'll close the bargain," said honest Walter, with vast satisfaction. "Only remember, my little lady, we must be in earnest. No fuming when I do my duty—I like strict discipline. No frowning, nor the shadow of one of those queer grimaces, or I shall certainly resign the appointment."

CHAPTER VIII.

"I weigh not fortune's frown or smile ;
    I joy not much in earthly joys ;
I seek not state, I seek not style ;
    I am not fond of fancy's toys ;
I rest so pleased with what I have,
I wish no more, no more I crave."

JOSHUA SYLVESTER.

IT was an enervating, oppressive afternoon. Several sets of the hotel
visitors were playing croquet at the same
time, and frequent little disputes and
much talk came from their plot, near the
shrubbery. More groups were seated on
the grass, or on benches, along the shaded
house-wall, if they were elderly and suspicious of damp, in spite of dry weather;

while a few slow riders on the Stray were
trying to imagine they liked exercise, notwithstanding the heat; and some flies came
occasionally past at a crawling trot, raising
little clouds of dust. In the background,
the windows on the ground-floor of the
hotel were wide open, affording varying
views of sitting-room interiors. That of the
Higginses, for instance, showed a tempting
display of five o'clock tea, a luxury not in-
dulged in by everyone, and which caused
some interested mortals to begin suddenly
confidential topics of gossip with the
daughters of the family, close on that witch-
ing hour—a practice voted "mean" by the
widow, who was aware that her misdeeds
and antecedents gave the principal piquancy
to conversation at these entertainments.

Huntley was leaning on the garden
railings under a tree, smoking one of the
few cigars allowed him by his doctor, with
keener relish for the enjoyment, and watching some one with a look of lazy content-

ment. He felt in an especially happy mood, perhaps from having been much employed, in his walks to and from the wells, in chewing the cud of very pleasant reminiscences of the past ten days. During these—since their quarrel and reconciliation—his strong pity and protecting fondness for his little Goldenlocks, as he had at first laughingly called her to himself, had changed into a restless dissatisfaction, unless he were always near her—increased even from that into proportions whose sudden growth would have surprised himself, had he thought about it.

As it was, he thought only about her. I think none other of womankind had ever before so filled his mind with one image, and he had none of his men friends here, nor any work, to divert his thoughts. He was so unused to women, too, that Mabel seemed thereby a hundredfold more bright and fresh, while her singularly infantile looks made him deceive himself longer into thinking this merely a strong fancy for a harshly-treated, winning child. In fine, he had thought of her and for her, and of how to please her, during most of the past livelong days.

Her sunny-haired likeness succeeded in holding regal sway over the kingdom of his mind, waking or sleeping; whether our side of the world were passing through darkness, or had grandly rolled round again into day and sunshine.

She had come out a few minutes ago, as patient watching of the door from a distance had made evident, and had seated herself near an arbutus bush, carrying Mimi, Madame's Persian kitten, the one living thing that lady was known to be fond of. (She had just desired Mab, with a petty tyranny which gave herself infinite pleasure, and was not likely to cause open rebellion,—speaking through her thin lips with smiling coldness, —to take out her pet for fresh air, and not to venture away from it.)

Meantime, he watched her, purposely dallying with the pleasure of going nearer. At that moment Miss Mawkesworth came past, all a-flutter with ribbons, flounces, and stray, fuzzy tresses.

"Oh, you naughty, naughty Captain Huntley!" she said, gently shaking her croquet mallet in his face with engaging archness. "Don't attempt to talk to me—now don't!"

"Certainly not, Miss Mawkesworth," answered Wat, startled from a pleasant reverie, but with ready acquiescence. "It is my duty, as well as my pleasure, to obey you."

"Horror!" playfully ejaculated the distracting damsel, with mild reproach, drooping her head more on one side, and softly regarding him. "You know you never came to help me into my pony-carriage this morning, though you were close by—quite, quite close. No, I shan't forgive you—at least, not just yet," she continued, with sweet ruthlessness. "I have asked somebody else to play croquet with me."

"Pray forgive me. I feel so unhappy," answered our friend, but with a look of happy relief that rather belied him. "Or, at least, tell me who is my favoured rival?"

"Why, he is"—with an innocent little laugh, and tremulous eyelashes—"he is the Rev. Sidney Seraphimus Smith."

"Smith—most uncommon name! And pray who may the reverend gentleman be?" rudely broke in Juliana Higgins's voice from behind, startling the heiress from her pretty posing and her confiding utterances.

"I don't think you know him, dear," she said, eyeing the speaker with pitying superiority. "Such an inspired man! I would introduce you at once—only, unfortunately, he is so *very particular !"*

"Keep him to yourself, my dear. I don't know him—but I know his brethren!" and Juliana put both hands in her jacket pockets, in a manner implying preparation for the

contest. But her enemy turned away, perhaps duly aware that her mental resources
were very unequal to the foe's powers of
retort, and trusting to the disdain expressed
in a raised chin and a peculiar sweep of her
retiring skirts.

Wat, meanwhile, looked on with the
utmost impartiality, and began to think
matters rather amusing.

"Sweet man indeed!" went on Juliana,
with a sniff of pity.

"What a simpleton she is, to be sure!
I've seen the personage—waves his hair
with tongs every night; sleeps in kid gloves,
no doubt; and displays a diamond ring—
so!"

Then, turning on her heel, and whistling
up her terrier, she departed with a more
manly air than is often attained by some
meek masculine spirits.

Poor Juliana! Probably she merited
most of the disparaging remarks then being
made against her by her late opponent, and

uttered with dull reiteration.   She was often vulgar, and sometimes loud.   But the downright honesty which made her see things and people as they really were, speaking of them without pretty euphemisms, but with impolite truth, saved her in great measure from ways of thought and action reserved for other circles than those of the Higginses.   If mushrooms, these latter had at least sprung from honest, hard-laboured soil, and were more wholesome than useless fungi.

And as any drift-wood may betray a current, so her short outburst against High Church curates might still point to an early love, once,—to push metaphor further,— like a streamlet, babbling pleasantly among green fields of youth, but long since merged in life's broader and more turbulent waves.

A late writer on civilisation tells us that marriage bears a fixed and definite relation to the price of corn; and so poor Juliana and a tall saintly-favoured curate had learnt several years before, when, on wishing to bring their joint grist to the mill, they found, poor young souls! that its amount was insufficient to produce enough loaves. Mr. Higgins had been far less rich then, not having made his last lucky ventures; had not cared to withdraw any considerable sum from his business to benefit one whom he secretly termed a "ritualistic priestling;" and hoped perhaps that his July would yet do better. One form of consolation, perhaps most often resorted to by men, is to fill the void left by some lost beloved object with the first stop-gap chance throws in the way. So, a short time later, Juliana (who had been fondly imagining her curate as more ascetic and self-renunciating than ever, preaching sadder yet touchingly rapturous discourses on the innate sweetness and beauty of humiliating self-denial), heard, with startled, sickening ears, that he had married the only daughter of a wealthy drysalter, having doubtless considered within himself that resignation shown in meekly

accepting the good things in drysalting pro-
fits which lay in his path, was fitter than
longer mourning after the unattainable.
Juliana, who had been rather a sentimental
though healthy manufacturer's daughter before, educated at a second-rate school, then
became the practical, bustling, noisily good-
humoured personage we know.

"How is it you are not with Mrs.
Langton?" asked Huntley of his new
pupil, in tones of happy, fault-finding patronage; having discovered, despite an effort or
two against it, that the arbutus possesses an
attracting influence over the human frame
impossible to withstand.

"I am free! I am free! and may talk to
you;" she looked up to answer, almost singing in gay, confidential joyousness. "Madame is engaged, reading devout literature
to poor dear papa, to quiet him."

"Why don't you listen, too? Very good
for you."

"Per-haps—perhaps, too, I dislike her

doctrines, out of opposition," answered Miss Mab (who had rather a turn for theological discussions), with a wicked little smile. " Do you advise Renan or Comte's works? (Those, however, are for papa's instruction; not that he has strength to follow —she herself prefers lighter things—novels, like the one you asked me yesterday not to open).

Huntley whistled to himself, and looked over the Stray. As usual, he had had the worst of that argument. In reality, Mrs. Langton, at that moment, offered a touching representation of a devoted wife, to any passers-by who glanced through the open windows. Her old husband was dozing in his chair, dreaming, it might be, of Upper Silurian formations, or perhaps of nebular systems, which dimly shaped themselves in his worn-out brain; but, nevertheless, she was steadily reading to him, in a monoton- ous, unceasing flow. Her thoughts were also far away; for, while eyes and lips were following the words, her mind was incessantly scheming and devising fine-spun little webs. But it was good to go on reading, since it kept him less troublesome; while her attitude was excellent—that pale, oval face, smooth hair, and the light-grey barege dress, with blue scolloped trimmings, being in perfect keeping with her *rôle* of gentle refinement. One might think Mrs. Langton, of Cherrybank, need not have tried so painstakingly to win the good opinion of those around her (for this was her present object). But the ex-governess overrated the social influence of some of her new acquaintance; and, perhaps thinking them good twigs to hold by during future bad weather, was spinning, and dexterously throwing, as many additional safety-threads as any out-of-door spider.

Some visitors had just arrived by the afternoon train, and the first sight of new-comers was generally hailed as an event by the loungers around; but neither

Walter nor Mabel took heed of it. Mabel, in terror lest the kitten should escape her, was holding grimly to it, though suffering from its claws, dug into her dress. She was also reflecting, however, what surprising thing she could do or say, which might have the pleasing effect of startling her Mentor out of his stupid reverie. He had lately grown far too much addicted to such; he would have called it a happy dreaminess. It was so pleasant to feel a little unlike other people; and safe, too, with him, since *he* never misunderstood her by thinking she wished to be fast. Only, unhappily, none of her brilliant ideas would ever come till about half an hour after the lost opportunity.

" Oh !" she suddenly exclaimed, a great sigh relieving her pent-up feelings, " do you never long to do something exciting?— anything to break dull monotony, and make one's veins tingle with life? If I could only ride, run, dance !—anything for the sheer pleasure of movement ! Not one person here seems to feel that, except—yes, there is a gentleman crossing the grass now, who looks as if he felt himself alive all over, and liked it."

The individual in question was a tall, handsome stranger, walking with a light and springy step—a man who looked the very impersonification of splendid health and perfect strength, from the top of his jet-black, almost too small head, to his active feet ; broad-chested, strong-limbed—take him for all in all, as good a specimen of a high-bred, athletic physique as one would often find.

"Dick Cust, by all that is wonderful !" exclaimed Walter, in pleased surprise. "What on earth can bring him here, of all men; instead of being at some deer-forest in Scotland? However, I am delighted, for my part, as now I shall have some one to talk to."

"To talk to," echoed Mabel, after a moment's pause, with a shade of disappointment. "Why, have you not—plenty of people?"

"By no means," said Wat, surreptitiously pulling the kitten's tail, and getting viciously scratched for his pains. "I understand neither coal nor cotton; iron, nor other commercial discussions. Yes! I suppose I ought to go now and see after old Cust."

He was not speaking naturally, but rather in a tone befitting one of the Blacks, when placed in such abnormal circumstances. But he was secretly uneasy, fancying that some glances were directed towards them by Mrs. Smith, his aversion. Perhaps he talked too often, in this gossiping place, to the child. She was not considered a come-out young lady, certainly. She was also in full view of her stepmother, who now even pointedly encouraged her to talk to him; perhaps in order to keep her from her father—yet—

"Why do you stay? You must want very

much to talk to a real friend," said Mab, with deliberation.

"How eager you are to get rid of me!—there is no hurry," he answered, with a reluctant laugh. "You must get to know Cust, though ; he is a splendid fellow. How much heavier and changed in looks he. is, certainly, since the years ago when I first met him!   Well, I am really off now. Good-bye—and keep a smile for me at tea."

This was in allusion to a tacit arrangement by which he always caught a bright glance as a good-night greeting, even when. not near.   If especially happy, it denoted that Madame had been more endurable than usual, and the French verbs a trifle less wearisome.

He was gone. She never even looked up, but she knew it; and then this poor little Goldenlocks felt sore. She seemed to see the cloud, no bigger now than a man's hand —his friend's—that might separate her and this kindly ugly man—first her playfellow, and then her Mentor. She told herself that it was quite natural for these two friends to meet gladly; yet she was already jealous of this stranger, who, unlike herself, had no doubt troops of other friends; who had also the great advantage over her of being a man.

Ah! none of them knew what it was to long for *anyone* to talk to—aged or middle-aged, young man or maiden; and she might, (despite new experiences) have possibly still preferred the latter; nor how very, very, weary it was to have grown up always apart.

It had grown dreary out there. In truth the sun had gone in a little, and no small, red Shepherd's Weather-glass, that daintiest of weeds, was more influenced by atmosphere than was she. By-and-by she wandered into the house, and passed the rest of the hours wearily enough, since she dreaded venturing into their sitting-room, and her own chamber was hardly a cheerful resort.

Life here was disappointing, after all; at home she would at least have been free.

It would be unfair to say of the little girl that she regarded Huntley with any of the unripe sentiment of school-bred young ladies of her age. Love, she firmly believed, was an impossibility somehow, till she should wear long dresses and bonnets, and be formally introduced into society, where she pictured herself as meeting with far more ideal beings than plain, prosaic Walter. Some of the ladies here had also given her strong hints that Captain Huntley's partiality for her was only attributable to her still being so raw and young, since he avoided all attentions to marriageable young ladies.

And Mab believed them implicitly—yet still! she was daily growing bitterly conscious of her old short dresses and unfashionable plaits, and would look at times, with a sincere envy which swelled her little heart, at older, well-dressed and pretty girls (how different from herself!) whom he addressed.

He was so kind. He treated her with respect, yet pity and good-nature, and never oppressed her with a sense of her deficiencies; and the poor victim of Madame's cold, smiling refinements of tyranny was intensely grateful to him.

CHAPTER IX.

"And I know, while thus the quiet-coloured eve
Smiles to leave
To their folding, all our many-tinkling fleece
In such peace,
And the slopes and hills, in undistinguished grey,
Melt away—
That a girl, with eager eyes and yellow hair,
Waits me there."

R. BROWNING.

THE longest Summer's day must come to
an end, however. That night, as
usual, the faithful Agnes was brushing out
her young mistress's hair, protracting the
task, since it vexed her heart to see Mabel
sitting there "desolate-looking and silent."
Then she lamented, partly to herself, with
her usual fluency of tongue, that her young

lady should have no enjoyment like the others in the house, "who were dancing away with the windows open, for it was a lovely night, though nothing of a moon, as, indeed, she and a French maid of a Mrs. Cust had gone to see, and——"

Here her talk was suddenly interrupted, just as she was pausing to take fresh breath.

A brilliant inspiration had flashed into Mabel's head. Acting on the impulse, she jumped up, telling her maid she no longer needed her. Accustomed to her vagaries, Agnes looked astonished for a moment; then, concluding that she had been dallying too long, and thus brought on one of Miss Mabel's impatient fits, she willingly accepted her dismissal. Besides, the fascinations of the valet of a certain Colonel Cust drew her strongly below-stairs. As her steps died away, Mabel listened; then quickly twisted up her loose hair with two dexterous movements, dressed herself hastily, pulling on an outdoor jacket, took a hat in her hand, and blowing out the candle, cautiously peered down the dim passage.

No one was in sight; so she hurried along it, and down the first stairs. Then came a similar passage, with two chambermaids like lilac-gowned ghosts, disappearing in shadow at its further end : more stairs—a turn to the right, where she came suddenly upon a hurrying waiter; then an open door, and then !—she was outside, and free in the garden, with the cool night air blowing upon her temples.

Ha ! this was splendid ! How gloriously free it felt to be out and alone in the Summer darkness, as of old at home. It was exciting—exhilarating ! And there was keen pleasure in knowing everyone else was mewed up within those walls, not dreaming how delightful it was out here, with a faint moon, and these deep shadows around. By day the garden was small; but this night it was changed into a vaguely moonlit space, from which rose scattered clumps of blackness, with here and there a mysterious, twilight alley, hardly resolvable into a gravelled walk.

At first her only thought had been to spy wistfully, from the shelter of a clump of laurustinus, the forbidden happiness of the dancing-room; but, stealing gently past the closed windows, she stopped for a moment beside their own. The temptation to peep in was irresistible: since this was the hour when her step-mother was alone, having rid herself of both husband and daughter.

Despite natural courage, Mab was growing to dread a good deal this cold Sphinx, whose change from her warmth in governess days gave the frank country child a feeling of mystery. But dread or no dread, curiosity was roused. The venetians inside were drawn down; but—yes—here, luckily, was one bar hitched up by accident; so, with a beating heart, brightening eyes, and cheeks flushing with enjoyment of the daring, she peeped in.

Little to be seen, apparently. Mrs. Langton was there, but she had her back turned, and was bending over a small, portable mahogany case of drawers on the far table. It was one the old man had insisted upon travelling with, and was supposed to contain some of his cherished geological specimens—though, in his jealous watch over such possessions, he let no other eyes see them. And now, what was Madame doing? —was she, too, peeping? At that moment she moved, as if to throw more light upon the case, and the watcher outside saw something in her hand—keys! And now —yes, now!—she was *trying them!* Mab set her teeth, and ground her foot on the gravel in her anger. Was even her poor old father's useless collection not to be sacred from the rigid, prying surveillance the ex-governess had established over father and daughter: against which she herself vainly sought to rebel, since Madame coldly told her she considered it a duty, and was never disconcerted when Mab surprised her in espionage.

Soon a smile came on her face, for Mrs. Langton had drawn back, and was examining, with a slight frown and puckered lower eyelids, her keys. Clearly her father had trusted his treasured minerals to no common lock, and Mab drew a relieved breath, watching now with amused exultation, since the burglary had so signally failed. What would she do next?

That was soon answered, for Madame unlocked her husband's writing-case, and, sitting down, looked, with keen, detecting eyes, over all the papers it contained; then thrust them back as if disappointed, but with carefulness. Apparently a fresh thought struck her, however, for, turning to the blotting-paper, she held leaf after leaf carefully against the light, studying the blurred lines with puzzled, close intentness, all unwitting of those other eyes angrily watching her outside.

Just then, bending forward in her eagerness, the rim of Mabel's hat made a slight
scratching noise against the pane; another
moment and Madame had stopped, yawned
a little, and was only sitting, with an air of
meek thoughtfulness, beneath the gas that
shone down on her oval, pale face and the
smooth hair she was gently sleeking down, as
was her habit. Next she calmly came to the
window, whereupon Mabel, in sudden terror,
made a rapid retreat, her last backward step
landing her full in the gardener's favourite
bed of double pink carnations.

From a safe distance she could yet discern
a shadowy outline standing before the blind;
then the latter was drawn up, and the figure
retired. After a few minutes of breathless
suspense, during which the hopping of a
poor little awakened green-linnet in the
branches which hid her, made Mab start,
she once more took heart of grace, and
crept forward with a determination to see
the end of her step-mother's strange actions.

That lady was quietly reading, with her dress gracefully spread around, and an air of serene blamelessness in her demeanour.

Mab paused a moment in irresolution; but, yielding to temptation, glided across the grass, glancing round in alarm as she approached the corner of the house. Then she saw long lights thrown upon the lawn from the brightly-lit dancing-room, heard the sounds of music and moving feet, and felt her own feet dancing responsively under her. It was too dangerous to venture past those lights. But, fortunately, her friendly laurustinus was near enough the windows to hide her, and help her design of seeing whether some one was among the dancers, and— with whom he was dancing.

At its further end, the large room was carpeted, and there the quieter folks were seated, playing cards, or talking and working. Nearer Mabel however the few people we know, and many others whom we do not, were valsing and whirling over a polished floor; and these her eyes eagerly followed, trying to single out various couples from the moving, changing crowd.

Useless quest; she could not see Wat Huntley among the dancers. Perhaps he was among the sitters, however, enjoying somebody's conversation too much to dance; while he, no doubt, thought her either yawning wearily over a faulty French composition, or fast asleep—(that was to say, if he thought about her at all).

Beside one whist-table was a gentleman with his back turned, talking confidentially to a pretty, invalid girl. Was that ?—yes, it must be he; and Mab's brows puckered as she gazed with wistful eagerness. He was turning his head, but it was hard to see rightly at that distance; she stretched her neck; then—forgetting all prudence, in her childish anxiety, made two steps forward into the light—saw,—and sprang back again into shelter.

How stupid! how dull! to mistake that

stranger for him, whom she ought to have known at any distance. She looked blank, and felt much ashamed of herself.

The dancers had lost their principal interest in her eyes, yet she still watched them from afar, seeing the tall figure of Colonel Cust towering over the others. Then a ludicrous thought struck her, of how they would stare, dared she carry out one of the many delightfully eccentric freaks which crossed what Madame called her "wild Indian" imagination. What, were she to spring in with one bound through that open window among them!—this tress of hair, which had escaped, flying loose—with her gipsy-looking straw hat too; which was probably on wrong side foremost?

She had made a loophole of observation for herself between the leaves; and so, with her head hidden like the ostrich, never heard a step behind her, for the rustling of the branches as she stirred them. But she gave a great start of guilty terror, as in the darkness a hand gently touched her on the arm.

Was it—Madame? Was it that most terrible, calm Inquisitress; from whose unceasing vigilance there was never escape?

Her heart was fluttering like a trapped, wild bird: her breath went till, with returning senses, she distinguished a man's figure beside her.

"Miss Langton!—what wild child's prank are you playing?"

"Oh! Captain Huntley, I am so thankful it is only you," was all she could answer in a glad, excited whisper. "How did you see me?"

"I was smoking alone out here, and saw you move forward into the light a moment ago. What can have brought you out?—at night, too? And I, who fancied you quietly asleep up there."

He pointed upward, and then flung away his cigar, as he spoke in a tone of chiding and deep annoyance.

Perhaps it slightly added to his vexation that he should have spent the last half hour pacing below an empty bower, weaving unusually romantic fancies, with tender thoughts of her in his honest, manly heart. While here she was out in the night on some mad school-girl's prank . . . but with him.

He led her silently back by the further walk, avoiding the grass under the windows.

"Don't be angry with me—*please*!" she said, in half alarmed, coaxing pleading: deprecating her Mentor's displeasure. "I wanted so much to see what you were doing, so I slipped out without anyone knowing. Then I watched them in there ever so long, but I could not see you!"

She was so relieved from fright, and so happy to be with him, that she never thought of concealing the gladness in her voice.

"Foolish child!" he answered—no more. But his voice too had changed, and something in its gratified, fond intonation made her silent; and they hurried on without a word into deeper shadow.

At the same moment—and when they had almost gained the side-door, to which Walter was bent on bringing her back without losing time—both stopped dead short.

Voices were heard, and figures came out from that door, crossing the open grass so as to pass near them.

"*It is—Madame!*" gasped guilty little Mabel, in such a terrified whisper as to be almost inaudible; and despite previous courage she trembled greatly in her nervousness. Wat caught her hand and drew it within his arm, then pressed it close, and still more closely to his side : so they stood waiting !

The figures passed by: a group of ladies, whose dresses brushed the grass with a soft, rustling sound. Mrs. Langton was nearest; but none noticed the silent figures in the deep shadows. All moved on chatting, till they went out of sight round the angle of the house.

Both drew a long breath of relief, but as yet neither uttered a sound.

"She is gone—we are safe!" whispered the little culprit at last; but so low that Wat had to bend his head closer to hear.

He could just see her eyes, in the darkness, looking up into his; could feel her soft breath on his cheek: some of her loose hair blew lightly against his shoulder and touched his face. Hardly knowing what he is doing or saying, he catches her other hand also, drawing her yet nearer to him.

"Promise me you will never do anything so foolish as this again?—promise me, won't you?" he whispered caressingly, lovingly; low as were her own words.

"I won't—that means, I do promise."

He could hardly hear that faintest of whispers, though they are so near: so his face bent still a little lower.

"That is right; dear little Mabel!" His moustache brushes her cheek; his lips touch hers. For one long moment both know not where they are—they do not feel that they themselves *are*! Their whole being and individuality seemed merged in each other; —lost to reality, for that second they had ceased living on earth!

Then, as if by mutual consent, both moved apart; and silent, dared hardly look at each other.

Mabel was trembling once more; now like an aspen leaf. The next moment, with a quivering gasp, she would have made one frightened spring away, but that Walter, who had partly recovered himself, seized her hand again with a firm, warm grasp; trying to speak in his usual kindly tone as he said, " Good night."

Then she darted from him through the shadowy doorway, and, hardly knowing how, gained her shelter. He, however, turned away, after one long glance at a well-remembered window, with the happiest smile on his face he had ever had, and the most feverish tide of joy through his whole

being, that he had ever known in all the
years he had lived. But Mabel pressed a
burning face into the pillow, feeling one
moment deliriously happy, and the next bitterly shamed at such wicked happiness : ap-
palled at her own mad freak and its terrible
consequences, and for hours weeping, wake-
ful, miserable, yet glad with some new
strange, bitter sweetness ; and she knew not
why.

CHAPTER X.

" Nous qui détestons les gens
Tantôt rouges, tantôt blancs,
Parlons bas,
Parlons bas ;
Ici près j'ai vu Judas,
J'ai vu Judas, j'ai vu Judas."

BERANGER.

NEXT morning our little heroine had to face her step-mother alone, with all the sense of her guilt upon her ; for her old father had had a bad attack towards morning. This illness, though Madame apparently made light of it, had given her cause for anxious thought, and planning, since dawn; and had greatly influenced the course she meant to take with regard to some suspicions of Mabel's late actions.

She had, when first she came as gover-ness, been obliged to toil with weary craft to gain her pupil's regard; then—when this scheming had been so unexpectedly crowned with success in making her mistress of Cherrybank, her subsequent small and very refined little cruelties, had been, in her mind, only a natural indemnification for the constraint she had been obliged to put upon her nature. And though she could never like Mabel, yet the latter's hot-hearted rebellion had no doubt prolonged and embittered the retribution.

But now! Should her old husband die sud-denly, and leave this hateful girl his heiress, she herself—heavens!—would be almost a pauper! Such another attack might end all—and never yet had she succeeded in hav-ing a will made in her own favour; despite hints, despite worrying, or even those coax-ing, maddeningly slow conversations alone. All was now difficult—*so* difficult! She must again abase herself to this saucy chit, and, above all, gain a hold upon her!

Her hands, which were large, and always. red with chilblains (the most unsightly features of her person), were busied with the cups, and in pouring out a weak decoction, called tea, of milk and hot water. Yet all the while she could see from under her meek eyelids; and her thin lips smiled a cold, mocking smile as Mabel soon pushed away her plate with a slight gesture of disgust.

The little girl seemed heavy-eyed and unrefreshed. In truth, she felt cold and nerveless; never before had she risen up to find the current of life flowing so low and chill within her. Sober daylight had washed all her late romance away, and left only unrest and shamefacedness. No doubt Captain Huntley had treated her as a fast, wild little schoolgirl, not as he would any lady; but she—oh! she felt a child no longer, and she could never look him in the face again.

Restless, yet strangely dulled outwardly, she got up to creep away unnoticed; but Madame, with a certain calm significance in her voice, which gave her hearer a guilty tremor, called her back.

"Stay, then, a little while, Mabelle. It will perhaps be necessary that we should have a leet-tle talk this morning—unless, indeed, you wish again for some fresh air in the garden!"

So she knew it all, then! For a moment the poor child quailed; but cowardice was new to her, and the next moment she bravely faced her step-mother. Was not this woman now always hard as ice to her?—relentless, grinding, despite that cold, gleaming surface-smile, which Mab dreaded as would a crew, drifting in lonely north waters, the prismatic reflections from glittering but deadly, blue cliffs? Her oppressor could be no worse; and it was her own feelings which made her so wretched, not fear of Mrs. Langton. Indeed, it was no new thing to feel somewhat like a hunted wild thing, tracked by a slow, yet untiring, unerring enemy; but experience taught her that Madame had a certain respect for her courage, when, as now, she turned to bay.

"She seems dangerous," thought the latter to herself, "it may be hazardous to speak; yet who knows what was not said to her by that ugly oaf last night? The old imbecile likes him too, and they might settle it all. Yes, yes, I must venture, but be cautious—oh! so cautious!"

So she said aloud, quietly, and with a more gentle, though an impressive manner,

"Nay, my child. Do not turn so hurriedly—you are nervous! Compose yourself, *petite*." Wherewith she began moving about, arranging the fall of the curtains, and softly disposing her books and knitting; each moment seeming an age, as she meant it should, to her waiting and watching victim.

At last she sank languidly into a seat, with her back to the window, carelessly motioning Mabel to another chair, where the light would be full on her face. Then, in a mixture of French and English which it would be wearisome to give literally, went on with quietness, that purring quietness so revolting to some finely-strung, sensitive natures—which now, for example, made poor Mabel's nerves shiver and creep.

"The time has passed, Mabel, when I should have asked you to listen to me as to your mother; for I am but too painfully aware you now only regard me as an interloper. Well!—it is perhaps natural; and if it has grieved me and irritated—often bitterly—does not now matter. I only ask you to listen, as to a woman who has had experience of the world. You yourself must feel it is my duty so to advise my husband's daughter, whether it please me or not. Choose yourself also, whether you wish to be considered as a child or as a woman."

"I am not a child any longer," was all those tightly compressed, soft lips could utter.

"*Bien*!   We will forget the child."   She paused a moment; but then her still slower words, freezing yet scalding, fell on her listener's heart, one by one, with terrible distinctness.   "If a child, it would be necessary to punish you for last night's folly—as a woman, I can only say, do you know what madness you have committed?   Nature gives most girls instincts of what is allowed—is modest; but for a very young girl to make a secret rendezvous in an hotel garden, alone!—at midnight!—with an almost utter stranger, of whose character and family she knows nothing — Mabel!   Mabel!   Could you not feel it was incorrect; was——?"

"It was no rendezvous!   We met by accident!"

She felt half-choked; her little heart was beating wildly against her bodice.

"By accident?   Mabel, I can depend upon your truth.   Are you *quite* sure?"

"Quite—I would swear to it, only you would believe me none the more!"

A little gleam came into Mrs. Langton's small, dull eyes; so far, so good. She went on soothingly, in a yet more subdued voice :

"For me, I believe you willingly; *but the world*!—Ah! poor child; you must be a very child still, not to know how they will slander and laugh and pull you into leet-tle pieces! Even Mrs. Smith, whom you despised, may triumph and sneer over what the proud Miss Langton has done!"

"Let them say what they please! Do I not know myself I meant nothing really wrong?" she cried, stung through every fibre of her proud soul.

"That feeling may console yourself, but not those who love you," immovably continued her tormentor. "Think a little of the grief of your sister when she hears this gossip!... and your father, who is so proud and particular; but, alas! now so feeble!—It would kill him: break his heart!"

"Don't tell him! Promise me you

won't?" the little one suddenly gasped, with a great dry sob, seizing her arm. " I will tell Maud myself—she will believe me —only *don't* tell him! Unless you are cruel, you need not say one word. Those other ladies never saw me last night—you are only trying to frighten me!"

For a moment her stepmother's lips were viciously compressed, and she pushed away the girl's hand. Then she controlled herself and spoke again, passionless as before; as if she had absolutely no personal interest in the matter.

"Have patience, Mabel. I am not cruel —I do not wish to frighten you; but since I could see, why not they? I said not one word to them. I wished to shield you. But later, when they whispered together, I saw smiles and sneers on their faces. I will not tell your father, either—do not thank me so rapturously. I acknowledge I keep silent for my own sake also, since I dread the consequences upon his health."

A silence followed. Poor Mabel never thought of distrusting her step-mother in this, as in lesser things. Did not this strange new unrest of her own feelings, the alternate gladness and misery of last night, and an inward whisper responding to some of Madame's words, seem to confirm the whole ? It was an appalling revelation that it was so fatally easy to commit errors in the world's eyes ! She had believed older folk were free, self-answerable, never misjudged ; as she would be too, after leaving childhood behind at Cherrybank. What had she known of life before but of living lonely and secluded, feeding her chickens, or dreaming in the rustling beechwoods above the dell ? She had read of, and could imagine, the strange pain in joy of those who killed, for the moment's pleasure, the dictates of their finest feelings. A weird disquietude, no more to be shaken off than their shadows; like these, ever growing longer, whilst they only sought to keep till late in the sunlight.

Had she, then, forgotten her pride—been unmaidenly; and was she therefore receiving just punishment? Her heart swelled bitterly with youth's rapid exaggeration of misery or joy. But her step-mother calmly and inexorably took up the conversation again; knitting with unslackening fingers, that made the little girlish creature before her feel as if one of the cruel Norns were weaving sorrow, evil, and misery into her mortal life.

"Believe me, Mabel, society is only one great, silent battle between men and women, each trying to get the best of the others, though all the while they talk and laugh or make love. In love, the man gains when he persuades the woman to believe in him, and show her affection; then she has lost, and the world laughs and applauds quite low, while he seeks a more exciting conquest. It is all a great farce, is love-making! And if you ever trust anyone, you will be very sorry for it some day."

"I don't believe it!"

The soft rebel lips unlocked to let out that one forcible protest ; but as Madame took no heed, she went on, stammering in her speech.

"You don't mean that—that *gentlemen* would try to make women love them, and then laugh at them ?   That cannot be true : some never would !"

How Mrs. Langton would like to laugh to herself in her unpleasant, mocking fashion ! But instead, she answered with all a matron's grave sageness and counsel.

"Most assuredly there is real love in this world—between *married people! Cela va sans dire!* But, before that, a man ceases to think seriously of any girl, if she returns his own liking, be it ever so tiny a little bit. He may amuse himself with her still, yet he says, low in his heart, It is cheap fruit ; I will wait for better. But why do I go on with this stupid talk to you ?" she exclaimed, interrupting herself with an affected laugh, and gaily proceeding in English, "You who are so young still, and who will wait till we match you

happily with somebody who is *grand et beau
et gai*! Bah! You would never so much
as let touch you with the tips of his fingers
this insignificant Captain of *cavalerie*."

Oh! wicked, guilty little Mabel, aware
of that terrible burden of a secret! "Not let
him touch her with his fingers," and he had
—kissed her! She put out all her self-
control with a mighty effort; yet, alas! into
her creamy skin there stole, despite herself,
a soft glow like the petals of an almond
blossom; coming and passing impercepti-
bly. Madame's small eyes noted this by a
momentary sparkle behind her dark eyelashes (far too dark these were to corre-
spond with her hair). Then, with a desperate
wish to end a discussion that seemed to
profane the most sacred adytum of her
pure young mind, the child forced her reluctant lips to speak again with steadi-
ness.

"You believe, then, that people here will
speak ill of me, because I ran out alone last

night, and so chanced to meet Captain Huntley?"

"Ah! dear child, I fear it. It is not what you did, but what they will think. Your only chance is to avoid him—always. Make light of his ugly features, and jeer a little; so they will think it all a mistake! And listen; you will be surprised, but we go with a party to Brimham Rocks to-day. I thought you seemed dull of late, and your father will be asleep all afternoon. This tiresome man will, unhappily, be of the party; but fear not, my child! You will show him he dare not boast nor laugh with his friends over——"

Mabel sprang up and stamped with a violence of impatience which made her own nerves tingle all over. It suddenly startled Madame into dropping a stitch, and sitting bolt upright.

"That will do!—that will do! I will be careful before these slandering, wicked people, for papa's sake! And as to what Cap-

tain Huntley thinks of me himself, who—
who cares?"

" Then go !—we understand each other—
and put on your habit at once, for you shall
ride !" as quickly retorted her stepmother
with unusual excitement, while her face
flushed dark red.

And Mabel went. Out from that torture-
chamber with a rush, and up the stairs; then
flung herself with one leap upon the bed,
burying her head in the pillows—grasping
the quilt with small but nervous fingers—
shaking with a wild passion as she raved
fiercely in half-stifled undertones.

"I hate her! I hate her! I hate her!
Oh! Maud, if you were only here—oh! if I
could only take back last night. Now they
will all know it; and he will never care for
me any more. Oh! *Walter . . .*"

Then even the stormy whispers died away
into dumb cries in her heart against the
wickedness of the world; against him for

cruelly forgetting how ignorant she was ; for having so hurt her self-respect.

But at the last they were against herself . . . against herself !

CHAPTER XI.

"It is the nature of the human disposition to hate him whom you have injured."—TACITUS.

AND downstairs, as soon as the door closed upon the girl, Madame too was suddenly shaken by passion; roused to unrestrained action by the quick leaping of the usually treacherous, slow tide in her veins. It is true, she rose quietly to her feet, and looked once all around, with the wary suspicion of instinct or long habit. But then! —with one quick throw her knitting was flung right across the room; and in her turn she pressed her long, thin foot on the ground with a prolonged hiss of anger.

"Ah, little wretch! Traitress of a dwarf!

Wicked and ugly that you are; *petite monstre* of sin and rebellion! Do you think I cannot stamp too? I can! I can! Do you dream I shall always sit by, cold and calm, while you alone grow excited—insult me? Wait a few months: only wait!"

Then she grew quieter, and stood awhile thinking to herself. What an inspiration it had been last night to creep and listen at the girl's bedroom keyhole, after she had heard some one at the window: then to have softly opened the door and found the bird flown! But for that, she would never have fancied outside she saw dim figures under the trees; nor have hurried back, making an excuse to her friends, thus spying Huntley alone. And Mab, the simpleton, believed that the other ladies had really seen her. *Bête!* Madame had not discovered much, either, as to the relations between this little witch of Endor and her male friend. Ps-s-s-s! —how she would punish her for this secrecy some day! And he?—ah, he followed her

with his eyes—perhaps thought of her fortune.   But as yet she believed he had said
nothing—was too cold-blooded or too hon-
ourable : whereat she laughed.

It was folly to say such feelings did not
exist.   She knew human nature better, and
had studied his; but what a blessing that
such foibles and weaknesses never oppressed
her!   Heavens! was it not?—for else he
might work so easily upon her old dotard,
who had taken such an unaccountable fancy
to him.   Were such a thing settled before the
old man's death, Mabel's husband would no
doubt watch over the will,—perhaps defeat
Madame's own plans utterly.   The doctor
had so strongly hinted to her yesterday, too,
that her husband was fast breaking up : and
how tender the idiot had been in breaking
it to her; while she seemed hardly to realise
what he said, so that he left her at last with
a very sober, even sorrowful air, and a pitying look as he pressed her hand.

The great mistake lay, surely, in not

having made the old man settle something on her at the marriage. But there!—had it not been difficult enough to force him to it; despite her devotion during the illness; despite his great weakness, and sick-bed doubts in leaving his only child almost alone; despite her own expressions of devotion to the latter—added to her tearful but utter inventions of village gossip concerning her care of him? Had his brain not been greatly unhinged by that fall, so that she had acquired a power over him similar to that of a keeper over a timid, crazy being, she was aware he would never have done it. And she hated him for it in her cold, patiently-cruel way.

She hated them all, and England, which reared them—its climate, its customs, its mock piety and hypocrisy of virtue,—ah! *how* she hated them! But had she not been taught since childhood to wage secret warfare against society and its existing laws, moralities, and religions? How she would astonish these moral, humdrum Quakers,

dared she just once burst out with her real
sentiments, and scream for joy when she
thought of their future ideal Community!—
their glorious World-Republic: when she
pictured herself dancing on the smoking
ruins of all that was now falsely called
holy; beating down the soul-throttling
tyranny of over-fed Philistinism!—the grinding oppression of proprieties! Yes, she de-
tested everyone in these British Islands—
execrated everything——

Just then a Persian kitten crept from
under the table; gently rubbing itself against
the cover before it advanced, with feline
slowness, drowsily purring and arching
itself.

"All but you, Mimi; my joy, my consolation, my only friend!—all but you!" And,
in her frenzy, she caught up the little
animal, and pressed it to her cheek again
and again.

CHAPTER XII.

'If I were poor and weak,
  Bankrupt of hope and desolate of love ;

.   .   .   .

Then would I freely venture, sweet,
To cast my soul down at thy feet.

But being not weak nor strong,
  Cast in the common mould of coarser clay ;
Sure 'twere to do thee wrong ·
  To set my humble homage in thy way,
And cloud thy sunny morn, which I would fain
Keep clear and fair, with my poor private pain."

Songs of Two Worlds.

WALTER HUNTLEY had not thought lightly either of that meeting in the garden. The first moment's madness over —the self-surprise, yet great joy,—he had paced up and down his room till late—had awakened early, and thought his thoughts fairly out. Now he knew all of a sudden what he wanted—had wanted for some days, without the strong wish taking definite shape till now,—and that was little Mabel for his wife, despite her youth and all his own drawbacks. Why not? Who cared as much for her, when her stepmother seemed to hate her, and her father was perfectly indifferent? True, he was only a younger son, with no looks, and few prospects, to recommend him; still he was aware of his good family, and most likely these Langtons were no better off than most small squires..

But, despite his strong love, it was not his nature to be rash or impetuous in thought which prompted action. Fairly, honestly, quietly, this sudden great change in his heart and mind, and perhaps whole life, must be considered; and Mabel's welfare and wishes must come before his own. She was so young! Would she really know what love meant? It was possible she might give him a childish "Yes," only to wish, later, that she had not been so precipitate—had waited to see more of the world. (Poor child! for her sake, he would so gladly have been handsomer, richer, more worthy of her.) Again, he might have frightened her last night—and he now blamed himself greatly for having so allowed his more animal self to get the upper hand. How differently he would have set about it had he understood himself sooner—would have tried for her liking with humble and devoted painstaking, instead of mere kindly patronage—would have shown her all the reverence he felt for the child-woman, instead of last night's rough wooing. But to-day would make plain whether he had only startled her into dislike, or had gained ground. All would depend upon that!

He was surprised and very glad therefore to accept an invitation sent him by Mrs. Langton, to take a seat in her carriage for a pic-nic to Brimham Rocks; and only when the party assembled, found—that Mabel was riding.

Madame had not arranged her party without care; for secretly longing though she was after any society or dissipation, to relieve a sick-room life very different from former gay Bohemianism, yet she was wary.

The Higginses, she knew, had lately bought a fine old country-seat, and talked of spending next season in London; and these signs of wealth, not the genuine goodness of heart of the whole family, made old Mrs. Higgins so dear to her. Miss Mawkesworth was also rich, and *might* be useful; while it was owing to Juliana's insistance that she had been forced to allow Huntley to be invited too. Miss Higgins had also asked a certain Colonel Cust to be of her riding-party: Madame thought little of it, having only been told he was one of the most popular of fashionable men.

This pic-nic, however, was quite eventful

from two causes: one being Wat's resolution above recorded; the second, that Colonel Cust and Mabel met for the first time.

What is much pleasanter than a gallop on a warm, breezy Summer's morning, away from town and all the glare of busy streets: what than riding along, a quickened and gladder self, over springy stretches of roadside turf, the wind in one's face having just swept over one of the highest uplands in England; while around stretch for miles and miles great pastures and thick woods, rich meads and low rolling hills, which seem the very heaped-up fulness and plenty of this goodly Yorkshire land?

Even poor Mabel forgot her late sorrows as her horse kept stride for stride in a brisk canter with that of a tall, handsome man beside her. For Cust and she had left the rest behind like specks on the dusty ribbon of the road, since they clattered out of Ripley and down here to Lurkbeck. None of the

other ladies would venture to ride her little
horse, which had frightened them, before
mounting, by some vigorous kicks; so a slight
difficulty was settled when Mabel offered to
get on.   Cust had admired her pluck, and
when the animal proved somewhat fresh,
rode on beside her for fear of accidents.

His little companion had, perhaps, never
before in her life looked so attractive,
though on horseback she always felt happy
and perfectly at home. There was a flush—a
tender glow on her face ; a proud, shy defiance of manner added to suppressed excitement; while late tears only made the angry
fire in her eyes soft and luminous.   In truth
her young soul had been passionately stirred,
and strange new thoughts had given her a
somewhat similar beauty.   He watched her
riding with silent, but surprised approbation ;
admiring in his heart the child-like, supple
figure, with its softly rounded outlines, sway-
ing in her saddle just enough to show the
grace of ease.

Cust was essentially a man of the world, sated with the pleasures which society poured out prodigally to him. Yet, though a warm welcome and brightening eyes awaited him at more than one deer-forest in Scotland, he had refused all invitations, in order to visit, for this week, an infirm old woman—one on whose life-dial time seemed to go back several degrees when sight of him gladdened her eyes.

This morning he had supposed that only a strong flirtation with Juliana could have relieved the boredom of the day. His was an old experience in it, though none believed that his heart had ever yet been touched: only he himself perhaps remembered one long-past attachment.

Talking to this fresh, fair child was different, he said to himself—and better. Her spell of an untaught, high-souled nature, added to a look of youth and infantile innocence younger even than her years, worked upon him too as it had upon poor Wat.

There was about her besides a shade of
recklessness, and at other times a sudden
change to subdued sorrow, which charmed
his fancy. So Cust put out all his powers to
please her; and few women or men either
had ever long resisted the influence of that
voice and manner; added to the strong life
in the man, and reckless high spirits, which
he knew so well how to tone down at times,
with the stateliest deference of manner. Soon
he knew a good deal about Mabel's life and
loneliness; whilst she, poor child, in her new
terrible wisdom of the pitfalls dug by men,
fancied she was sagely reticent: never
guessing she was only filling in a highly-
coloured, pathetic outline given him by
Juliana.

He liked her for that pride better than
ever. And what was it—a trick of voice or
manner—which seemed to stir fleetingly,
but would never awaken, faint memories of
a dreamy time long-past?

Now they were riding between the high

sand-banks of a steep, wild lane which dipped below abruptly into a shaded hollow, whence rose red-tiled and fluted farm-roofs; with the gleam of a gravelly beck under the bridge, and darker trout pools beneath the trees.

"I have answered my catechism long enough," cried Mabel at last, after his final questions, flinging aside her newly-imposed trammels of more than conventional restraint, with the frank, mutinous gleam in her eyes which poor Huntley knew so well. "It is your turn now—why did *you* come here?— What do *you* do?"

Cust laughed, and from habit drew closer.

"Are you too young to know that a woman is at the bottom of every reason? I came here to see a—lady! Don't be shocked; she is both my grand-aunt and god-mother."

"I do not in the least see why I should

P

be shocked," she simply answered, looking at him with clear eyes.

"Nor I either," he said, with a slightly graver alteration of tone. "And as to what I do —it is much easier for a little lady like you to be amused here than such a great, big, stupid man as I am." Then lightly again: "You might hear me my Watts's Hymns instead of my godmamma. Pray do! You have no idea how nicely I can say them—No?" as she shook her little head, while it amused him playfully to tease her. "Then let me turn teacher."

"Worse and worse. Miss Higgins said yesterday you could only teach one thing ——" She stopped short, ashamed of her betrayal.

"And that was flirting, I suppose? Don't listen to any more naughty stories about me, please. But after all does not a little of it make this old world pleasanter at times?"

Some evil instinct prompted him to try

her, and his dark, handsome face looked inquiringly in hers: looked with a glance that had done execution before now, and a peculiar smile as he carelessly rested one hand on her horse's back.

"By Jove!" There was a sudden swerve, a clatter, a dusty vision of horse heels before his eyes! and when he recovered himself the little quadruped was snorting with angry satisfaction, fully shared by his mistress, while Cust could not but laugh. Yet she answered him, shame-faced at venturing on such a subject, but too proud to avoid it,

"I know hardly anything about it; but— if it means any sort of falseness or pretence, I think—I would rather never know more."

" And long may you think so," said Cust, with a look and tone that at once restored her equanimity; respecting the woman-child who had been brought up in grand old Nature's lap, far from those who call evil good and good evil.

They had grown then far better friends than prior to this interruption, before the smell of heather came; and by-and-by the sight of it in great brown flats, springy and damp, with stray clumps of violet blooms. At places it sloped into still darker brown water-courses, scooped in the black peat-soil, or again crowned the low ridges against the sky-line. The breezy air, the moorland scents and associations, all made the sportman's soul leap up within Dick Cust; while Mabel looked all round, drawing long, free breaths.

And now appeared the rocks, piled in such strange confusion on the crest of the upland as if flung there in Titans' rough horseplay!

"Like a great herd of petrified Mammoths or Mastodons," she cried to Cust; and he, feeling he was rising to the unusual occasion, answered with stately gravity, "How small and weak we men feel at times, after all!"

Then they rode up alone together, and Cust lifted her down.

How was he to know that Walter Huntley had waited half-an-hour for that poor chance? No matter; the latter came forward with a bright smile on his sunburnt face, which changed, poor fellow, as Mabel turned coldly away, after the barest of greetings. He hesitated, as if about to follow her: she felt nervous and frightened. But at that moment Miss Higgins rode eagerly up, calling to her; and then, jumping down, seized and drew her aside some way, "for a sound scolding."

"To gallop off like that, with the one man I wanted specially for myself!—after all my entreaties to Mrs. Langton to let you come! 'Sorry?' Oh, I daresay—but it's too late now," she grumbled self-pityingly, with grim humour. "I did try to pound along the road after you, but my horse knew better, my dear. I must say, though, you are a promising young lady; and won't gossip be going soon—oh, wait! just won't it?" (Poor Mabel stared at her in dumb, wide-eyed terror.) "For a child like you to choose the two nicest men here is a lesson of wisdom to all of us; while as to Captain Huntley, we all know——"

"What?" in blank desperation.

Juliana, who had taken a pity and a great fancy to the child, looked at her in surprise: then good-naturedly answered,

"Nothing, dear. Only my stupid nonsense. Come and sit beside me at lunch." And Mabel obeyed; but she was very uneasy in mind.

Somehow they divided into groups round two rocks serving for tables. Walter had resolved within himself to go where Mabel sat, but was begged by Madame to find a shawl; and when at last it was discovered that she had accidentally seated herself upon it, the circle there was closed. Mrs. Langton sweetly made room for him, however, between herself and old Mrs.

Higgins, who was innocently admiring the Colonel, and his politeness to Mabel. Strangely enough, Madame never looked: in truth, hardly noticed Cust's appearance; but then she had her hands full, detaining Wat—though he could see it all.

"Dear me! I never saw her looking prettier, Mrs. Langton; and how the Colonel seems taken with her!"

Cust was already *the* Colonel to this worthy old soul.

"*Si belle qu'on l'appelle Mabelle,*" smiled Madame, whilst watching Huntley's face. But Wat never moved a muscle, though he recognized a hidden sneer better than she thought. The moment afterwards, when he turned away to open some champagne, he did look black—but only a wasp spied that!

All the rest of the afternoon, while wandering among the strange rocks, he never for one moment got free from Madame's vigilance. At last he fairly succumbed to it, in the forlorn hope of pleasing her.

Just once, however, after long waiting, when Mabel was last to come down from the rocking-stones, he stoutly turned to join her; speaking as best he could (with his new feelings) in the old friendly tone.

"I have not had one word from you all day, have I; how is that?"

"N-o? Ah! I have been talking to everybody, you see."

"Except to me," he said, with a poor attempt at a laugh, which failed in being hearty, and which she fancied slighting. "And yet I did think a little—it may have been very conceited on my part—that I had a certain claim upon you——"

"*None!—none!*" she almost passionately interrupted. "How *could* you have any?"

"Only as being an older friend, I was going to say," he quietly answered, deeply stung and pained at her tone, which to his heart seemed the bitterest of reproaches. "Only as that."

"Because I met you first, should that prevent my making other friends later?" she cried, the flush still vivid in her cheeks, with a strange tremor through her; while his quietness still misled her—was it ironical?

"'Prevent you?'" he slowly echoed. "Surely not. And you may even get to like them—better. I only trust—I do trust —that you may know your own mind."

At that she glanced up at him, in wonder and half fright; then suddenly caught the pained, fond look, the strange light, in his eyes—paused one second in trembling irresolution; then frightened, sprang away.

A minute later, and she was safe with the rest, trying to cover her confusion by pulling desperately at some tough heather, and so hurting her fingers. Dick Cust at once hastened to help his bright-haired little moornymph; then, despising the really withered blooms, insisted, despite the entreaties of everyone, on climbing up to a cleft in the rocks where were fresher purple spoils.

Madame was not present.

Old Mrs. Higgins, however, screamed and shut her eyes at the danger, as he drew himself up the bare, high crags; but between times she unclosed them to peep, exclaiming in an ecstasy of frightened rapture,

"Oh, dear, dear! he'll be dashed to pieces, like the poor babes of Israel! But, girls! —it's worth coming twenty miles just to see so beautiful a sight!"

Even Huntley mentally thought him the finest-made man he had ever seen. In honest envy he contrasted his own inferior animal powers with that powerful, sinuous frame, whose every movement betrayed such flexile, supple ease of strength; with the small head, which (as the old Greeks have taught us) befitted a Hercules. He seemed thoroughly imbued with such full, keen vitality; of a truth in his superabundance of life lay his powers of great attraction. And these lines of Browning's came into Walter's mind:—

" Oh, our manhood's prime vigour! no spirit feels waste,
Not a muscle is stopped in its playing, nor sinew unbraced.
Oh! the wild joys of living! the leaping from rock up to
  rock—
The strong rending of boughs from the fir-tree— . . ."

Soon they started homewards. To Dick Cust it seemed natural to ride again beside his little companion of the morning; but his friend thought it only *too* natural as his carriage passed them.

As for our foolish small maiden, there was to her a certain glamour, feverishly over-excited as she was, in this handsome Colonel's implied homage; and part of the attraction lay in the reputation she had vaguely heard from the Higginses of his wickedness. Well, she felt wicked too! And perhaps he was as maligned as Madame darkly hinted she herself soon might be. In fact, she was in a morbidly excitable frame of mind; and any intercourse might have been in a lesser degree acceptable which helped to banish self-questionings about Huntley. She would not think of him;

Madame's knowledge of their meeting was too horrible—yet she felt so weak! Even Cust's air of strength seemed to give her a vague moral support; while his manner soothed her, and his real liking flattered her innocent vanity. So they had grown very confidential before they got back.

Yet, even after all this new friendship, when he once spoke with a smile of the pleasures of society to which she no doubt looked forward, he was startled by the vehemence with which, rousing herself from a dream, she cried,

" I believe life has nothing but disappointments—nothing!"

He looked at her in astonishment; then caught some glimmering of the hot, defiant nature and restless little heart.

"Heyday! Come; you must not take such ideas into your head, my dear little lady, because some few things have gone wrong in your short life. Believe me, there is plenty of fine weather ahead."

And she, who had been thinking of the old loneliness of the almost deserted home— of Madame's iron rule later, and now the troublous present—was silenced, and a little cheered.

In her own room the first sight to greet her was a parcel addressed to herself. Books only—scientific and a little dry; no present, surely, to arouse any strong emotions. Yet Mab caught up the volumes to her breast, and hugged them lovingly; then put them down, ashamed of her own transport, but again fondly touched and looked them over and over.

Walter was outside again that night; but with little inward gladness now, as he looked up at a certain closed window. And then a wind leaped up far off with a troubled sound, and blew on and on towards him, ghostly and weird and cold : before it reached him, the chill seemed already to have passed into his heart.

CHAPTER XIII.

"But had I wist, before I kissed,
That love had been sae ill to win,
I'd locked my heart in a case of gowd,
And pinned it with a siller pin."

Anon.

MABEL had slept off much of her trouble; yet, next morning, her faithful attendant kept hinting, with some uneasiness, that she was not yet "quite herself." Mab tried to satisfy her care-taker; declaring that a bad dream was the principal cause—"A horrible dream, that I was following a funeral. What does that signify, Agnes?"

Hitchcocks was at once interested. If she possessed one gift without the shadow of doubt above her fellows, she was pre-eminently oneirocritical. So she employed herself in demonstrating that, by all known laws of dream-lore, a funeral signified a wedding, and begged earnestly for further particulars. But her little mistress was now silent.

She could not tell how she and a certain tall, handsome man had been dream-riding wildly over shadowy fields, till, slackening ever, they had found themselves slowly following a hearse; nor of how she had awakened sobbing heavily, despite the great oppression of sleep, because that black funeral-car held the remains of Walter Huntley : her only friend two days ago, when she felt still a child—now one whose name, even in thought, made her cheek hot, and troubled her with doubts and misgivings hateful to her nature. But she had resolved to keep up a stout heart to-day, and try to face, without cowardly terrors, whatever good or evil might be in store for her.   Hey ! how reviving to feel brave and fearless again !

Suddenly, to her surprise, Hitchcocks coughed ominously, and began, with reluctance and solemnity—

"Excuse my takin' a liberty, Miss Mabel; but as there isn't no one else to give you advice—seeing I take no account of them that only knows nasty foreign ways,—from what a certain person let slip, haccidentally-like, about the gentleman he is with —though very nice, but wild-like—and had another name—the which he only changed when he'd run through his fortune, and got another from old Mrs. Cust's husband, as is below stairs (leastways, she's below stairs, but the poor old gentleman is below the ground)——"

"In the name of all that is mysterious, Agnes, whom do you mean ?"

"Just Colonel Cust, m'm," gravely answered her monitress; with the consciousness of satisfactorily fulfilling what she considered a momentous duty. "Which is a liberty, in warning you that he had another name, and played—so they do say, though a real gentleman—that, had Mrs. Lester been here——"

"I know—I know. Well, my good Agnes, she soon will be here, so make your mind easy. Till then, I—won't play cards with him. Now I must go."

But Hitchcocks followed her hastily, drawing a well-thumbed little book from her pocket, and running her finger down the index.

"To dream of Milk! Cherries! Flying!— no, of *Hanging*!" (in a joyful tone). "You didn't never dream of hanging, Miss Mabel, dear?"

"No—never," answered the little mistress, in a tone of thanksgiving, as she escaped from the room.

"For that signifies elevation above your present pursuits——"

"Rather more than would be pleasant,"

came, in answer, from half-way down the stairs.

"—By marriage!" finished the Sibylline Agnes, leaning over the balusters to deliver this parting information down the well-staircase to the second landing.

Then, returning to arrange her smart cap before Mabel's glass, she reflected, with calm self-approbation, that it was but right some person of experience should guard over her young lady's interests—who fitter than herself, that had carried her as a baby? And she gave a little sigh at her secret heroism in telling Mr. Bennet at home twice lately that she could not marry him (nor set up at the " Apple-Tree "), to leave her charge alone, exposed to Madame's tender mercies, till after—*the Death* !

She shook her jaunty head mournfully over the event which prescience told her was impending. Maybe after that the poor dear might live with Mrs. Lester, and be happy. Meantime, she had promised Mrs.

Cust's Mam'selle and the Colonel's Mr. Lawrence Delany to go for a country walk the very next Sunday that ever was. Perhaps the latter's manners might make Bennet uneasy—but there! Bless him, he needn't ever know nothing about it.

Downstairs, old Mr. Langton was still lingering over his weak tea and thin toast, daintily breaking the latter with trembling fingers. The cool grey light fell on his scanty, yellow-white locks, and searched in vain for a speck of dust on his exquisitely neat black clothes. Meanwhile his eyes were ranging over the table-cloth in an idle dream, yet minutely noting every wrinkle or stain with faint disgust.

The action was somewhat emblematic of the man's whole life. Timid, fastidious, with tastes and senses most easily offended, he had always sought to escape in silence and reclusion from all that jarred upon his fine sensitiveness, while that close searching into details was his greatest mental characteristic.

Of late his studies had been principally geological. But they had been varied and many, for always he had concentrated his powers upon subtle, minute and ever more infinitesimal investigations; then had wearied—sickened of the task because others snatched the crown he was labouring to deserve, so turned vainly for solace to knowledge in other branches. Analysis was to him the one great vehicle to convey hidden, guessed-at truth to minds; but, his intellect once narrowed down to the requisite microscopic smallness of subject-matter, his eyes were fastened there; his doubting brain with weary wariness distrusting and weighing again and yet again apparently certain inductions.

He could never raise himself from that stooping, endless examination of atoms. He could never, as it were, expand his chest freely, taking a broad, general view of the

vast known, or only dimly seen workings of
force and matter; wasting, repairing, destroy-
ing, renewing; embodied now here, now
there—nor looking at the earth's great whole
with wiser, enlightened eyes, after the knowledge yielded up by those integral particles,
had boldly deciphered—as those before him
did, and others to come we humbly believe
yet will—another page written long cycles
ago in the great hieroglyphic nature-book of
Truth.

From the end of the table his wife silently
amused herself by tracing what resemblance
she could between him and Mab (who, in
spite of her weight of care, had still an
appetite for breakfast, of which the little
girl felt ashamed). The same shy defiance
in both; but the grace in the girl was weakness in the man. The same coloured hair;
for in his, though whitened, the warm glow
still lingered, like a last tinge of sunlight.
But there resemblance ended, for the young
girl's frankness and warm impulses of gene-

rosity or hot indignation were all her own.

"I feared you would have missed me yesterday, dear friend," she insinuatingly observed.

"No; oh, no; by no means," answered poor old Miles Langton, with unusual haste. "I—I slept, and studied. You are too good." Then his gaze fell on Mabel, and he asked with a slight interest, "And with whom did I see my little girl riding back yesterday — was it yesterday? Soon she will grow too old—eh !—to ride alone with gentlemen."

"It is the Colonel Cust, my dear, an ex-officer of the Guards: a very quiet and properly thinking gentleman, and steadie; but so steadie!" answered Madame at once, with a smooth glibness which made Mab, in mute astonishment, broadly commit the vulgarity of staring.

"Ha, ha, ha! Well, that is good! Commend me to you for a character, Mrs. Langton—when I want one. And good morning to all of you!" called out Juliana's hearty voice from the open window behind Madame, where she had just familiarly looked in; then she sat down on the sill and put her head into the room. "He would be delighted to hear he was so quiet and nice, I am sure" — (*sotto voce*—"It would be so new!")   "Don't stir, pray!" as the old man tried to rise and greet her with cold but scrupulous courtesy. "I'll tell you all about him, Mrs. Langton, if you like. His name is Richard A. E. Newland Cust, for I hunted it out yesterday in an old Army-List. Newland used to be his name, you see, till he came into a fortune and added the Cust."

A momentary silence followed.

"Pray speak less loud, dear Miss Julie; I have such a headache!" Madame said, with a gasp, covering her face with both hands; a great shake and irritability in her voice, which she vainly tried to control. "Do you —really know this about him?"

"Know! I know every blessed thing about him." (He might have doubted that fact.) "Long ago he was only handsome Dick Newland, and rather a scapegrace. Once, when he was quite young, he nearly ruined himself in Paris; but this old Mrs. Cust's husband left him a great deal."

"Yes; he told me how fond she was of him," Mab was chiming in—when Madame made a sudden movement. There was a crash; for she had upset the cream jug. The old man began muttering feebly, but angrily, for now he could seldom restrain his annoyance; while Mabel tried to set things to rights, and Madame herself endeavoured, with a troubled face, to apologise. "A thousand pardons; but when Mabel speaks so loud *cela m'agace les nerfs* !"

"You are greyish, certainly!" said Juliana, with unrefined bluntness, looking full at her. "Let me advise you to go and lie down; and if you are not in for something nasty, like scarlet fever or small-pox, you may be very thankful."

Madame, with unusual dulness of retort, only answered that the advice was perhaps good. Then, repelling an impulsively good-natured offer of help from Mabel, who was bewildered at the unusual occurrence, she left the room; while the old man, too, disliking strangers, crept away.

"You will have no tasks for to-day, at least, you poor little midge!" observed Juliana, with a great yawn, in vigorous tones, which could be heard in the story above. "Heigho! Cust—Dick Cust! I like the name. Why! what on earth—is that?" for a faded rosebud fell lightly just then in her lap, and as she looked up and around in astonishment, a voice from the window directly above—where was the individual in question—said, "And so she likes it, does she? So glad!"

Mab, though she could not have been seen, sprang back like a scared fawn; but

Juliana, who considered herself too old to mind such a *contretémps*, only laughed at her own discomfiture more loudly and heartily than usual.

Upstairs, after locking her door, Madame stood, propping herself with both hands against the table; looking with a blank face in the glass—a very frightened face—and there was a peculiar shiver in the muscles of her back. After some long moments she recovered herself—moved dully; then dragging forward a chair heavily, sat down, and let her head drop into her hands. And her thoughts ran somewhat as follows:

"Fool! fool! To be beside him all yesterday and never to guess it! Even brutes have more instinct of danger, and as to affection—I could have sworn to recognize him *always!* Certainly he is changed ... then he was so slight and beardless, and only two and twenty. The name, too—how did we never hear of that down in Jersey?

Changed ! yes, yes . . . but could he suspect—— ? "

She turned, and looked long and anxiously in the glass ; then seemed somewhat
re-assured. " Courage ! Sometimes I verily
believe I am a coward at heart. There is
less risk in this than I have often run before
in the old days, and *exulted* in it ! Even
should he recognise me, he must keep silent ;
for his own sake !   Dare I try to escape ? . . .
Yet to remove my influence from the old
man now would be fatal—and the doctor has
told several people that these waters are
necessary for his life.   What an outcry if I
took him away !   No ; I must keep close
for a few days—then hurry to London.
Why am I so unnerved ?   But what I lost
—lost ; such a man ! and riches ! position . . . !"

She rose at last, and rang for Hitchcocks
to pull the blinds, and to bring her Mimi.
Upstairs the said Mimi had seized the opportunity to fling down that handmaiden's

workbox, and hunt her reels, making a network of thread round the chairs; from which delights she was speedily torn by the wrathful Agnes on her return.

"Drat you for the tiresomest, plaguiest," (shake! shake!) "worritingest of little brutes, you!" Then, in the demurest of prim tones, "Here is Miss Mimi, please m'm."

So the curtains were drawn softly, and Madame lay still to recover from her severe headache, while Mimi, at her shoulder purred, and, it might be, soothed her.

CHAPTER XIV.

"I have walk'd the world for fourscore years;
 And they say that I am old,
That my heart is ripe for the reaper, Death,
 And my years are wellnigh told.
It is very true; it is very true;
 I'm old, and ' I bide my time :'
But my heart will leap at a scene like this,
 And I half renew my prime."

N. P. WILLIS.

LATE though it was, almost eleven, Dick Cust only now entered old Mrs. Cust's room for breakfast.

What a warm—too warm—but cosy little room it was; metamorphosed into a boudoir, for the time being, by the still beautiful old lady, who sat there in state: Silvery curls falling on each side of her withered, but none the less striking patrician face; those brilliant dark eyes piercing through all who approached her. The light came through rose-coloured silk blinds, which she always had put up, wherever she might be staying for some time. The scent of flowers seemed heavily to weight the atmosphere. Two canaries were singing with distended throats, while the tables were covered with photographs, freshly-cut books, the latest inventions in needlework, and sketches too, for those old eyes and hands were still capable of a skill which might have shamed her grand-daughters, had that ancient beauty had any. She was breakfasting now on a cup of chocolate and a small roll, while her French maid stood deferentially behind her.

"Good morning, grannie. Late as ever, you see; but you and I suit each other to perfection in our habits," was Cust's cheery greeting as he entered.

Stately though she was, yet the proud, clear-cut features of that old lady relaxed and brightened wonderfully at his sight; then she dismissed her maid with a haughty condescension, which would have won praise in the palmiest days of the Faubourg St. Germain.

The Colonel seated himself down to the breakfast prepared for him especially, and was eyeing his eggs with a gaze of healthy hunger, as she answered, in a tone which implied reproof was useless,

"You will never mend in anything now, Richard. You are too old, my dear boy— though it sounds unpleasant to say so; yet," she musingly continued, as if fairly considering the matter,—"yet I own you are a good type of the generation—strong, healthy. Polished courtesy, of course, belongs to the past; still you have a certain air beyond others. I have remarked that even high-bred animals possess something similar."

Her grandnephew heartily thanked her for her agreeable morning remarks upon himself; and while making raids for food, was understood to observe that she perhaps granted more to him than could be said for their ancestors, since he doubted whether possessing much that was good had ever been a striking characteristic of the New-lands—excepting good looks.

A little wicked laugh in her old black eyes reminded one of an occasional similar, but more reckless, gleam in his; while, notwithstanding her stiffness, one guessed that the generosity, staunchness to friends, and fascinating high spirits which made him such a pleasant, easily-forgiven sinner, were part of the good and evil inheritance transmitted to her also, as for generations to all of their house.

"Yes—at least, we had all handsomeness and courage."

Almost involuntarily, and with a smile which deprecated her vanity, that old lady slightly arranged her silvery curls with a withered hand loaded with emerald and diamond rings; then went on, with more vivacity,

"But in features you have not kept up the family reputation, Dick—though I admit your head is not ill-shaped, and is small (a sign of energy in my mind, let them say what they will). But your face was never strictly handsome, my dear; in fact, it is almost *broad*, which is generally fatal. No matter. I really believe you are *worse than handsome* !"

"Worse!" He burst out laughing. "Who upheld me stoutly through good or evil, as long as my memory goes back? Grannie! grannie! you have much to answer for. Had you let me go to ruin long ago, you would have been rid of all my misdeeds, and of a blot on the family beauty."

She laughed too—a low, indulgent laugh. Truly enough, she had scores of times fought his battles when her husband declared, in anger, that, despite his own weakness for that handsome, wild young scapegrace, the cup

Perhaps her education in France, in her dim, past youth, was to blame for such leniency. Perhaps, again, she recalled so many sins and follies of dead generations of Newlands, that she could well overlook his hot-headed errors (of which losing and lending money with fatal ease were the greatest), or consider them but the necessary sequences· to sharing that bluest of blood. Or was it the secret attraction which such prodigals have for many women, who will again and again grant them a brimming measure of forgiveness—a tender interest —which steadier-going, correct folk sadly often fail to awaken?

Things which might be ugly nearhand look so different at a distance. But what possesses almost a fascination for some, when viewed from behind safe fences, may also be imagined as far more terrible than the reality by other timid souls; and these, in the back-swing of changed opinion, may fall into the more dangerous error.

Cust's grand-aunt was generally wiser in the wisdom of this world than that of another; but it had been weighing upon her latterly to give him what moral counsel she could. So, according to her lights, this heathenish old woman tried to fulfil the duty.

"Don't think I wish to preach a sermon, Richard: you know how contrary that is to my ideas of good-breeding. Still, of late, I have found myself regretting greatly that you have no longer any occupation—any ambition—to give you real interest in this dull earth of ours. I am an old woman now, and I have seen that the pleasantest men in society—those, in fact, who try to escape the duties, and take merely the pleasures of life—only succeed up to a certain age. There is no use in struggling, Dick; one must grow old and respectable. The mere appearance of being useful is then such a help to us, my dear. Even growing turnips, or rearing shorthorns, would give you a certain weight—a solid reputation—in the country. And then, you are not even married."

She was watching keenly the effect of her words; but, unhappily, just at that moment he turned away his head.

"Neither a useful fellow-subject, nor even the head of a household—eh?" he answered, with slight awkwardness, aware he must not too quickly change the subject. "In fact, grannie, though you would not hint at anyone's age for worlds, it is true that a few more Summers' suns, as the penny-a-liners say, will see me——"

"Nonsense! You are in the prime of life; you have enjoyed your youth and freedom—what better time could there be to marry?" she gaily interrupted. "And to you the only difficulty will be whom to choose amongst so many."

Was that really all? He might have told her something more; but at all events he did not. He rose instead, pretended to yawn, and then lounged to the window. By-and-by a new current must have come to his thoughts, for he said, in an altered and cheery voice,

"By the way, grannie, you must see that little Miss Langton I told you of. You like young, pretty faces about you—and she might brighten the time."

"She is pretty, then? Yes, my dear. I remember her mother too. Poor, but good family—oh, very good."

Cunning old lady! She was quite startled at the glaring connection she saw between his remark and her late counsels.

"Pretty? Well, I hardly know, though her hair would have delighted Titian. A shy little girl; but, at times, she has a strange attraction one cannot explain, quite distinct from beauty or cleverness. She might have it were she downrightly plain."

"And the most dangerous gift she could have!" There the musing old lady stopped dead short. What had she said? Was this the way to foster any faint signs of matrimonial thoughts in his mind—signs she had vainly hoped for during years?

"I must be doting!" she thought, in a rage with herself and her septuagenarian failings; then continued with suspicious suavity,

"Not that I should think too much of that, my dear Richard—certainly not. No doubt if this little Langton girl were married to—hum—well, anyone handsome, and well off; and—let me see—not too young; for, when men have little experience, they are not indulgent enough—"

He laughed heartily.

"That will do, grannie. Let us sincerely hope she may be so fortunate. And good-bye for the present—I must be off now."

CHAPTER XV.

"The diamond,—why, 'twas beautiful and hard,
  Whereto his invised properties did tend;
  The deep-green emerald, in whose fresh regard
  Weak sights their sickly radiance do amend;
  The heaven-hued sapphire and the opal blend
  With objects manifold: each several stone
  With wit well blazon'd, smiled or made some moan."

                                      SHAKESPEARE.

THE cool grey morning had grown chiller
and damper, till now in the afternoon
there was apparently in the prospect only
wet below, heavy vapour overhead, and a
moist atmosphere of fog between, through
which came down a cold, continuous rain.

Huntley stood by an open side-door; he
had come there meaning to take a solitary
walk, in order to think the better. The sight

of the weather outside prevented that; but he still remained there, leaning against the doorway, and lost in thought. Poor, honest Wat Huntley! In every situation of life heretofore, that demanded serious reflection, he had always inwardly felt, with a certain sturdy self-reliance, that at last he should see the one right course to lead him to success. Now every man not in love was wiser than he : even most men in love too, for this was the first time with him during his full thirty years, and that fact alone bears strong significance.

He felt as one in a maze ; or in a strange atmosphere, where ordinary things had suddenly and softly become invested with different meanings; and most meant—ways, means, or times of seeing Mabel. Since the night before last—how long ago it seemed !—his eyes were as opened. Her every former little tone or light laugh came back now with new, strange intensity. Surely, surely no other child, or fair girl, or woman born,

had ever before been so fresh and sweet—
so wrongly neglected, with a forlornness that
went straight to his heart; so—— There
was no use in arguing the matter—he was
wholly, utterly in love !

But how best to approach his little way-
ward darling; that exactly he did not know.
Yesterday he had simply enough hoped
to re-establish their former relations; and so
beginning afresh, by tender, patient devotion,
make winning the more certain. Then her
manner had showed, as he thought, that she
understood his love; and was frightened,
and even angered, child-like, by it. It never
could have entered his mind that she fancied
he had been trifling with her; for filled, as
his whole being was, with love for her and the
novelty of his great wish, he felt as if every
passer-by must now know his secret, and
read an offer of marriage in every line of his
face. Since their meeting in the garden, she
must know it too. And if she gave him
no opportunity of asking her yet awhile,

it could only be because she *would* not.

His honest, sweet-tempered self again got the upper hand as he leant there.

" I'm not of much account, anyway; and if I become as morose as a bear, it will hardly add much to my charms," he said to himself, with a kindly humour which could play upon even his more troubled situations in life, lighting their one side, and which proved the possession of a truly sweet and healthy mind.

He had taken the poor little thing by surprise (and himself too); but he must just hope, and give her time to get used to his ugly face. There was Cust, though. He, too, had eyes; he had seen and admired the child, as everyone must. What would be the end of that? What, indeed, would be the end of the whole matter? He only knew, with a positive, if vaguely-based inward knowledge, that he could make the little one happier than anyone else ever would. He would never try to startle the child into fancying she loved him; but neither would he yield one inch to Cust or any man—all between them was fair in love and war.

He heard the shuffle of weak, aged footsteps coming, and turned about. It was poor old Mr. Langton, who, seeing Huntley, his friend, stopped, looking from under his brows with a pleased, but painfully timid expression. The shyness of even his manhood had too evidently passed into the constant trembling fear of an unhinged mind. The circle of his life was fast completing itself in the sad stage of second childhood, almost as it had begun.

With a quavering voice, but still a courteous manner, he asked Huntley to come and sit with him awhile. And though failing to recall Wat's name, he remembered not having seen him for two days past, and said so in a tone of somewhat querulous reproach. Wat pacified him as best he could, and went with him gladly; but as he passed the room belonging to the Higgins family, he heard laughter, and thought he recognised one voice.

Too true! The Langtons' sitting-room was empty.

"My womankind have left the room to myself. Quite a—quite an unwonted luxury, ha! ha!" said the old man, with a strange chuckle, as he motioned Wat to draw up beside the fire, that his own feeble circulation of vital powers rendered necessary, even in Summer. "Mrs. Langton is in bed —with headache."

Wat had felt called upon to echo his host's laugh of childish pleasure; but his own was of the feeblest, no more mirthful than Lucifer's under the Devil's Bridge, when cheated of his prize.

Mr. Langton was now gently staring into the red, warm glow behind the bars. Having vague ideas that Wat shared heart and soul in all the theories and varied topics of thought which hour after hour displaced one another in his own brain—an idea engen-

dered by our friend's general silence, but
kindly acquiescence whenever such seemed
expected of him—he began a monologue, as if
to his other self, embodying his ideas about
new discoveries through deep-sea dredging.
By-and-by, encouraged by his listener's apparently silent attention, he had not only
plunged to the beds of the oceans in discourse, but, coming safely up thence, passed without apparent connexion to the
realms of philology and ethnology; seized
illustrations of theories he forgot to explain
from all quarters of the globe; and finally
mined, in tremulous fits and starts, down to
the lowest strata of the Paleozoic period.

Becoming peculiarly sleepy, and with a
titillating, soothing warmth in his toes about
this time, Wat, lying back in his armchair
before the fire, grew only dimly conscious of
observing, "Quite so. Yes—yes. You
and I agree, sir," whenever a specially long
break in the speaker's monotonous, quavering tones occurred.

Gradually the old man's discourse low-ered into an undercurrent of indistinct mutterings, coming to the surface only in one excited word or so; then dropping again into the old subdued key. Once, in the twilight of his mind, he startled Wat by imagining he had stumbled in his person upon an adversary, as to some opinion of his own relating to crystalline schists.

"You differ from me, sir . . . differ? Ah! I am feeble, and my intellect is un-grateful—slow to my call. Yet I will listen to you patiently; even for hours—weigh every tittle of evidence you adduce, and——"

"Heaven forbid," thought the luckless Walter; and hastily waking up he said aloud, "You mistake, sir! Differ from you? —not for worlds! Why, your arguments for the last hour have been quite unanswer-able." Which, as he had never been able to catch more at the loudest moments than a mumble, sinking again into voiceless gestures, was after a fashion true; and the poor old man smiled with senile pleasure, soon rambling again into other dim fields of knowledge. However bored, Wat could not find it in his heart to vex him by leaving. He sank once more into partial somnolence, lasting perhaps half an hour ; during which he had dreamily made friends again with Mabel, nay more! induced her to listen to him with a smile, faint, dawning ; and—and then at last !

He started wide awake, to find old Mr. Langton standing over him whilst feebly holding by the mantelpiece; mysteriously showing in one shrunken hand a small key that was attached round his neck.

"You wish for it?... Ah! well, well. In general I suffer no other eyes to see them. It would pain me to let malign influences approach my little treasures." He laughed with a feeble effort, and uneasily looked at Wat. "But—but you have been my friend here, young man—appreciative; yes truly !... and to be trusted. as are not women—so let it be. Yes, you shall see them! . . . But a few gems and small; yet good of their kind; and collected by my own hands during many travels."

Wat, who had been wondering of what, on earth or under it, his aged host was speaking, now had a glimmering perception that the late muffled tones which had refused to pass the half-closed portals of the lips, had some reference to mineralogy. He accordingly gravely screwed all his features into an expression of most wise mystery, to match the look of secresy with which old Langton gazed fearfully round, keeping one hand on a small mahogany, steel-bound case that stood on the table at his elbow. He even observed furthermore that certainly women—especially housemaids—were the very mischief for tidying whatever one wished left alone.

One more peering glance around! Taking the cue from his elder, Wat even eyed with severe suspicion the curtain-folds, chuckling to himself over his own new and wonderful talent for humbug. And then the key was turned, two secret springs pressed, and the door of the strong case flew open, displaying a row of shallow drawers.

The topmost one, labelled "Quartz," was full of fragments of mineral; some un-interesting enough to Wat, even though the old man dilated lovingly upon each one as he drew them softly from their cotton wool. This was an agate ball, lined with crystals of amethyst. He had himself picked it up in Auvergne; and he laughed quite aloud, his childish mirth dying away in a quaver, as he pointed out how the violet colouring was deepest at the points of the crystals.

"The old port, you see—gone to their noses."

With equal interest he went over the other specimens and varieties of quartz, rock-crystal, and silex; cairngorms, jaspers, and chalcedonies of various shades; a large cornelian, whereon the head of Pallas

Athené was exquisitely engraved; a bit of pale girasol quartz, which, when held to the light, showed a rose-flushed, growing to blood-red, sunrise deep in its heart; and one rare piece of white jasper veined with crimson threads faintly imaging a human hand. But at the last, Walter did give an exclamation of hearty praise as he espied six glorious cat's eyes—the most beautiful he had ever seen—hidden apart.

"Ah! you recognise them—*châtoyant* quartz; yes—bought by myself from some Cingalese, who had already cut them *en cabochon;*" and the old man chuckled as the other looked in wonder at the brown beauties gleaming so felinely at him, while he broke the tenth commandment in his heart.

Drawer followed drawer; and, despite real admiration, Wat found it difficult to coin new phrases for lauding a little collection of Gamahées on agates, simulations of birds, fishes, and trees—felt almost as helpless when a bit of crimson tourmaline was given him as men do when expected to admire a baby ; though, to save their dull lives, they can't think what to say under the circumstances.

He thought he had originated quite a happy thought by observing that a fragment of soft-hued blue felspar, prettily mixed with flakes of silvery talc and white quartz, would make a fitting ornament for his host's daughter. But the peevishness he evidently evoked considerably damped him ; the old mineralogist's face wrinkling at once in the most sinister and extraordinary fashion even his lips protruding with the vexation that, like most emotions, now had the upper hand of its former master. His guest wisely put a bridle on his own lips after that ; even when seeing a heterogeneous drawer of pale pink coral, flawless amber, snowy pearls, and sunny Oriental turquoises. Yet he opened his eyes somewhat over that marked Corundum.

Was this old man so rich, then? For no trifling sums could have purchased that small but brilliant show of gems—all varieties of sapphire, Oriental rubies, emeralds, topazes, and aquamarines. He could scarcely praise them for thinking how bravely they would flash out from some warm-tinted tresses, clasp daintily, with pride in their glow, one young white throat, or, pearl-like, gleam softly from the small faint rosy shells of certain ears.

But one drawer remained, towards which whenever the old man's fingers had mechanically strayed, some after-thought seemed to restrain them therefrom.

"Shall we not see this last, Mr. Langton?" asked Wat.

There was a hesitation on the part of the other; his timid glance shifted uneasily to either side.

"This!" he faltered—"this! To my guest I can refuse nothing; but—only some few uncut diamonds. (She is safe upstairs, though," he added, under his breath); then, looking pleadingly at the younger man as he hurriedly drew it out— "As a favour, pray look quickly! Do not delay—some one might enter!"

There they lay, on their soft, white beds; two or three really beautiful uncut diamonds, and many smaller ones, like mere crystal in their present dulness. But, beside them, a small gold ring; and the miniature of a sad, beautiful woman, with dark, shadowy hair.

Wat half drew back, feeling guilty of impertinent intrusion. As if relieved at his lack of closer curiosity, the old man carelessly pointed to a pair of glorious deep-blue sapphires.

"Dark, eh? Male sapphires such ones were therefore once called—a quaint conceit!"

In the gesture his hand lightly touched them, and the coat-sleeve raised slightly the layer of cotton-wool, unwittingly giving

Wat one glimpse of something of parchment below, that somehow suggested a legal document. Hardly a glimpse, for the door-handle rattled, and, with an alacrity which made Huntley doubt his eyes, those trembling hands had shut the drawer, closed, locked the case, while their owner turned to face the intruder, with anger, yet pitiful nervousness.

It was Mab, the sweet, fresh face of poor little Goldenlocks, who, seeing all at once Walter's presence and her father's annoyance, would have gladly sprung back; but remembering she was too old for such flight, had to come forward, looking apologetically at the latter.

"I beg your pardon," she said, "I thought you were alone; and—and, that you might like—might not mind, perhaps, if I kept you company meanwhile."

If the humble speech to a parent was somewhat touching, far more so was the mute appeal in her eyes, only to let her be of *some service to him* ! Wat felt all through him that in the other's place he must have held out his arms to her. But the old man never saw it. He was half sidling backwards, crab-like, towards his own corner, and what between nervousness and annoyance at the exposure of his fright, answered with bitter ceremoniousness,

" I thank you—I thank you. But pray, in future, never leave your more fitting occupations on my account. All my life I have preferred solitude—I do so still."

She caught Walter's look of pity, but her unreasonable little heart only leaped up in sudden anger against him. What right had he to range himself on her side ? As if her father—who would be yet recognised as one of the greatest scientific and learned men of his age—did not know better when such feeble chatter as hers would break in with discord upon his musings ? (It was not jealousy that Wat's society was preferred by her father before her own; yet she would

have been jealous somehow had others been
so favoured.) Meanwhile Wat had his opportunity; and, leaning against the mantelpiece, did not know what to make of it. He
only asked her where she had been all day.

"I have been spending the whole afternoon with the Higginses."

"Indeed! Well, I hope you had a really
pleasant day," he heartily said, glad, at least,
if she had enjoyed herself.

"Immensely so. Nothing was wanted;
and *of course* we amused ourselves, because
Colonel Cust was there."

It is a great temptation, when we have
just been snubbed ourselves, to let any wit-
ness present see how she or he likes the
feeling; and Mab would not have been
nearly so sore at her father's coldness had
Wat not witnessed it all.

"That must have made it delightful!"
said he, gravely; it was so new to him to
speak in (secretly) bitter irony that his own
words sounded queer to him. Nothing

wanted! no one wanted! Not he, of a certainty. And yet, had he only guessed it, such little maidens do not always speak quite the truth, and——

The clock struck five, through perfect silence; and had an angel, as the German saying goes, been passing through the room, he would assuredly have seen two people in very hurt and irritated tempers. Or stay! Was a veritable angel, indeed, coming to stir the standing pool of their ill-humour? for just then the door was thrown open, with the announcement, "Mrs. Lester," and there was a vision of a tall, graceful woman in a dark travelling dress, who rustled towards them, holding out both hands as she came.

"Oh! Maud—Maud!" cried her little sister, with something between a gasp and a faint scream of delight; and she sprang forward to put her arms about her. Then ensued a rapturous greeting. Both forgot the others present, in their fond gladness, rapid queries, and as hasty explanations. Huntley was quietly busied in setting the table to rights, for Mabel's bound had pulled half the cover and the books to the ground: a dire vexation had the old man seen it. The latter was sitting quite still, however, and even when Mrs. Lester turned to speak to him with gracious sweetness, he only looked at her feebly, as if from a long way off, and dropped her hand without answering.

She turned towards Wat then, to whom it seemed as if a warm, charmed atmosphere surrounded her. Miss Mab, meanwhile—all the late past forgotten in the excitement and real joy of seeing her first good friend in the new, great world and Maud together—eagerly introduced them, according to a method of her very own.

"Maud, dear, this is Captain Huntley—a friend of papa's and Madame's; and "—in eager haste, as if impatient of her own delay—"and I shall tell you all about him presently. Captain Huntley, this is Mrs.

Lester—and you know I did tell you all about her already."

Neither could help looking at each other with some alarm; then Mrs. Lester said, with a sunny smile,

"You have, at least, the advantage of me, Captain Huntley, in Mabel's description of ourselves. Let us only trust she was, and will be, merciful to our failings."

How can one describe Maud Lester faithfully—describe her so as to make each reader think instinctively of the sweetest woman he has ever known? And yet not even that describes her, as some tenderly fair gleams and lights and tints can never be reproduced on canvas. Their thoughts no more make the warm, living being of flesh and blood than De Heem's or Huysum's flowers are like real Summer roses, whose soft wide-blown petals, unfolding to give forth sweetness, we can not only see, but also smell and handle.

She was no girl now, but a woman—tall,

large, graceful ; bearing her thirty years or
so with a grand and gentle stateliness that
seemed to all in her presence a thousandfold
preferable to the mere fresh-blown prettiness
of youth's insolent heyday. Without the
trace of a wrinkle, as if no frown ever crossed that low, broad white forehead, which
her dark hair shadowed in great waves,
defying braided glossiness. Her face was
neither oval nor yet finely-moulded enough
for strictly classical-loving eyes. It was even
far too massive about the chin to please
others. But still, in the beautiful curves of
her broad, sweet mouth ; the subdued fire-
glow of those brown orbs, large as were
ever ox-eyed Juno's ; and in that pure complexion, warmly-tinged as if one should stain
the smooth skin of rich, palest-brown fruit
ever so faintly with scarlet juice—there was
to many a humanly impassioned ripe beauty
far beyond cold correct loveliness : such a
beauty as the glorious full harvest moon owns
over the slighter silver sickles that precede her

advent. To look at her one felt of a certainty that here was a fair earthly saint; not raised stylite-like into too pure air for our grosser-breathing organs; but rather an Elizabeth of Bohemia, who, with her lap full of loaves for the poor, said, in her sudden cowardice, they were but roses she was hiding. A character faulty, truly; but, withal, most loveable.

> "Lean penury within that pen doth dwell
> That to his subject lends not some small glory;
> But he that writes of you, if he can tell
> That you are you, so dignifies his story."

CHAPTER XVI.

"A sweet, attractive kind of grace,
  A full assurance given by looks,
Continual comfort in a face,
  The lineaments of Gospel books ;—
I trow that countenance cannot lye,
Whose thoughts are legible in the eye."

SPENSER.

IT was Sunday next day—a garish, unpleasant afternoon; sunshiny, yet with
puffs of cold wind round street-corners that
sent the light, sandy soil in flying dust into
folk's eyes. Still, little crowds, headed by
fathers of families, were leaving the hotels
for long walks in various directions: the
elders considering this the wisest and most
decorous fashion of getting through what

was, to many, secretly a wearisome time till dinner-hour.

Mrs. Lester, however, had comfortably established herself in the Langtons' sitting-room. This gentle lady was in truth somewhat inert, especially since she had been living alone, and therefore under less inducement to exert herself. Not so minded was Mab, who sat on a low stool at the other's feet, her small but useful hands lying lightly in her lap, as with great interest she watched the groups outside come and go.

Looking down at her, the elder woman could not but silently acknowledge that Miles Langton's theory of upbringing had, at least, made his daughter as fresh, frank, and healthy a little maiden as you should easily find in all the west country. Sweet as wild thyme, strong and grateful to the senses as heather firm in gait. From the warmly-golden little head and apple-blossom face to her small but rounded and strong limbs (shaped in full curves of true beauty) all bespoke a training under the sweetening influences of warming sun and fresh breezes, far different from the cramped school-life of her many sicklier sisters. It was strong life that was leaping and coursing through her veins, even now playing in her muscles. For her feet were dancing secretly with the wish to exercise them, to be off to Harlow Hill, and feel the strong wind sweeping up towards her and round, then away over the levels below. But Maud chose to stay. While she so did, her little sister would also have staid quiet there till half cramped, rather than leave her side or lose one moment's talk—when a year's whole hoard had to be lovingly poured into those kind ears.

And few people were so pleasant to talk to as Maud Lester, she listened so well. For herself she had rather a gift of silence; but it was a warm, comforting, living-and-breathing sort of sympathetic silence, which together with her grand, perfect womanli-

ness of face as of mind, and slow, gracious
smiles, drew out confidences as the warming
June sun earth-hidden mists.   She knew
more than anyone for miles around her of the
half tearful small secret gladnesses and joys
of some, or of such troubles as have to be
borne by each heart that knoweth its own
bitterness; griefs that are the better for
being once opened out to kindly air, but
that it is a wrong to others to let spread
further.

All this while Madame was escorting her
old husband up and down outside, in the
least frequented, yet most sheltered path she
could find in the fields.   It was remarkable
how much she had kept her room all morning; and that at present a shady hat and
thick, doubled brown veil made her face
perfectly unrecognizable.

Mab was now gaily narrating to her sister
the smiling but deadly faction fights of late,
between Miss Mawkesworth and her party
on the one hand, and the Higginses on the

other, which she had heard of from the latter.

But Mrs. Lester seemed somewhat disturbed.

"Do you know, dear," she said, with the slight embarrassment she always showed when feeling constrained to point out a defect somewhere, "I don't *quite* think these people are right friends for you. No doubt Mrs. Langton does not yet understand the difference, but they can hardly be in a good set. Are they not terribly new?"

"*Brand new!*" laughed Mabel. "Juliana told me so herself. 'Bless you, child,' she said, 'everything old must have a beginning; and it's better to be that than not even *anything.*'"

Miss Langton was a little republican, heart and soul, without much knowing it. But without knowing it either, her sweet elder had been cast in that ancient mould of grand, gentle, yet immovable exclusiveness, ill-suited to the newer spirit of the times.

T 2

Not being an angel yet, Mrs. Lester had her little weaknesses like other folk. And one shortcoming was a lack of broad views, with regard to the old standings of families and to social stratification; so that whenever she met with those of a lower grade asserting themselves to her level, she was ruffled in mind. And considered such as a super-imposed layer thus exalted by a violation of the laws of nature and society.

"At least, one knows who Captain Huntley is," she observed, with some relief. "Huntley Hall has been theirs for generations. And besides being so gentlemanly, he has a most trustworthy look—the sort of man one thinks one might know thoroughly, and only like the better. You like him very much, little one, do not you?"

"Like him very much?" she answered, somewhat pettishly, twisting away her head. "I am not at all certain that I do. Why should you think so?"

Ungrateful child! Yet, the moment be-

fore, Maud's praise had sent such a rush of
warm gratification through her; and, this
very morning, she had been doubting
in her heart whether she were not misjudg-
ing kind, ugly Wat. Perhaps he had *really*
forgotten that she was not a mere child!—
could not guess all she now felt. And he
had seemed pained by her manner twice.
In truth, she felt deadly ashamed of the
strange liking for him she tried to smother
in her little heart—so different from any
careless fancy he could have. So Mrs.
Lester's question took her aback.

"Really I hardly know why I thought
so, my dearest. It was only an idea of
mine; and you know, Goldenlocks, my
ideas are very often wrong."

True enough, O Mrs. Lester! when such
ideas have been femininely reasoned out.
Old Mr. Lester would laughingly say his
wife was all heart, but no head; yet her impressions—or, rather, that strange intuition,
one of the grandest gifts of Providence

to women—were often startlingly true.

"But, Maud," went on her little sister, laying her hand upon the other's knee, who was stroking her bright plaits, "there is one gentleman here I do so hope you will like —I have been longing you should meet him—Colonel Newland-Cust !"

The white fingers stopped upon her hair. No breath sounded after one long inspiration, had she listened; and her cheek pillowed upon the other's lap, what should she see of the face above her?   But, to the older woman, with that one word, all the finely-balanced, interplaying vital functions of her corporeal nature, that had hiddenly and harmoniously worked in constant circulation or self-adjusting giving and taking, without stop or stay for days and years, were as if arrested by one sudden shock, and, for moments—how many she knew not,—motionless.

Then her heart beat again.   Breath came back to her, and quickened pulses.   And a soft gleam of great gladness swept over her face, as if she had thought to see the shining wings of the Good Angel who had brought about all her life's happiness, and her features had momentarily caught the silvery reflection. She softly said,

"I used to know him, dear. How long ago it seems!—and yet not very long, either. How things come back to one, as if they had only happened yesterday!" But, after Mab cried out in pleased surprise, Mrs. Lester somewhat hesitatingly added— "Did he never ask after me?"

Mab had to confess that he had not done so, and she felt real concern at his neglect.

"But never mind," she added, consolingly, and yet desirous of excusing her friend. "It is unlike him to forget, certainly; still it was a *long* time ago, you say—and think how many people he must have met since! And I did so hope you would be great friends with him, dear old Maud, for I do like him very much."

Blushing a little (it was that anyone could forget Maud, yet think anything of her!), she raised her head, to plead the better, looking in her sister's face ; but the other gently drew that head down again.

"How could I be vexed, darling? Tell me more about your friendship with him."

There was ever so slight a change in the brave voice.

So Mabel told her everything gaily. No faltering now in her rapid little tongue. No hot inward shame in avowing, with both admiration and some veneration, that this was the very incarnation of the ideal hero of her childish romances. Told how from the first moment she had thought he looked so handsome (and so brave) ; and of how he had paid her far more attention than to the grown-up young ladies, and differently too, "for he treats *me* with far greater respect !" At which she drew up her head with laughable dignity. And how he had brought her to see old Mrs. Cust, who had been so charming, and had kissed her when she left; while Miss Higgins had said afterwards—

"Yes, dear; what did she say?"

"Great nonsense!" and Mab, though talking of the ideal hero, laughed right out, like an amused child, without embarrassment, being very conscious of her short frocks and childish hair-plaits, which made Juliana's speech too absurd. It seemed even nonsensical to repeat it; though whatever Maud asked to know, she should know. "Well, she declared that old Mrs. Cust was longing for him to marry, and she said silly things about her sudden fancy for me. It seems Mrs. Cust's maid told Juliana's that the Colonel had never liked any girl—of my age, I suppose—as much. But perhaps that is because people here think me such a child still; and so my bad manners do well enough."

Ah! well-a-day! How changes come, and the baby Mab of yesterday is a girl—

and loved. How frankly and innocently the child said it all, too!

"I would not think too much of such things, dear: it hardly seems nice to learn praise in that way ... But I for one think my Goldenlocks deserves more than all the liking she may ever get." Poor soul! she hardly knew what she was saying.

Ah! sad, sweet face, that had thought one moment to look again into the sunny—to to each generation amaranth-flowering—fields of youth; the next, timidly drew back, sharply taught they were never again to be trodden by her, so turned that wistful gaze to see only the peaceful, solitary path she must always follow.

"Why, there he is! Look—look, Maud!" gleefully cried the once so timid little recluse of Cherrybank, springing to the window.

Out upon the grass was standing the Colonel; himself the central point of an admiring circle to which he was displaying

the feats of Jock, his favourite collie. The
dog looked like Cust's obedient genius, said
Juliana, as the beautiful black and tan
animal watched its master's face while
trembling with eager readiness. And Dick
himself, tall and straight as a fir-tree, tower-
ed kingly in their midst, and still, except
for a wave of the hand to the dog, or a
word, was not perhaps unaware of the eyes
upon himself also. Wat gave a grunt
thereat, under his breath; but then honest
Walter had always been plain, so was perhaps over-hard upon such small vanities.
Now Jock is bidden to hide, and tries to
writhe his hairy black body into the short
grass; quivering and wriggling. And now he
springs back and forward over his master's
stick, while all the ladies cry out with delight, as his silky coat waves backwards at
each still higher leap.

"Oh, you perfect duck!—you sweet
thing! I must kiss you—now I really
must!" lisped Miss Mawkesworth, running

forward, and prettily throwing herself down, to put both arms round Jock's rough neck; with sweet neglect of all her flounces, curls, and ribbons.

"Love me, love my dog!" audibly observed that rudest, most disagreeable Juliana. But Dick whispered something lower, whereat the fair one archly shook her head in reproof of his naughtiness, and, with a fond, sentimental gaze, dropped one chaste, butterfly kiss just over Jock's eyes.

Horror! The next instant a long, grateful, doggish tongue licked right up her blooming, but artless cheek, and screams of delighted laughter burst from the unmannerly Higgins faction.

The damsel delicately hid her face in a fairy cobweb of cambric and lace, and fled indoors for eau de Cologne, which, with a stifled sob, she declared indispensable to wash away the contact. Cust the next moment, however, spoke aside a few words to Mrs. Higgins; and then, with his springy step, yet stately carriage, came straight across the grass to Mabel's open window.

"Miss Langton, can I persuade you to come with us? Mrs. Higgins desires me——"

The words died upon his lips as he looked past her into the interior. But Mrs. Lester had quietly risen, and putting out her hand, said, in her slow tones,

"How do you do, Colonel Cust? We have been watching your clever dog. Perhaps you hardly remember me—years change one so much."

"They have not changed Mrs. Lester," he answered, in quite a low, quiet voice.

Man of the world though he was, all the calm self-possession required by Englishmen of high breeding was almost breaking away from his strong will, for he did remember her—only too well! For years he had not seen that fair face; but from the last time he reckoned the death of his best happiness, and the beginning of a new course of life, outwardly gay, inwardly without a kernel, and leading only to vain regrets and self-reproach. And yet the old sweet voice was calm as ever!

Not trusting himself for long to equal the composure he bitterly envied, he turned, after a few sentences, to Mabel; and the older woman saw this, and accepted her fate.

Just then Miss Higgins, impatient of the delay, came running up to Mab.

"Why! can't the Colonel persuade you to join us, child?" she heartily cried. "Do come—to please me. I always feel quite dull leaving you behind; so I waylaid Mrs. Langton, and she gave you full leave. We are going to see all the hot springs; and they say one well is real chickenbroth!" she persuasively added, apparently believing such an enticement was not to be resisted.

Mabel was quick-witted enough to see the serpent's trail in Madame's good-nature—meant to separate her from Mrs. Lester, whose influence the former dreaded. She bent back towards her sister, whom Juliana had not perceived, whispering,

" Really, I don't care to go. Before you came, of course, it would have been different; but I could not bear to leave you! Quick —say you would miss me!"

But, to her surprise, Maud hastily replied,

" It would be better to go, dear, if Mrs. Langton wished it. Besides, I have a most interesting book I shall finish. I almost think "—with the ghost of a smile—" it will be as amusing as your company, you vain little lady !"

Amusing!—God help her, poor soul, as she watched them out of sight, and then went upstairs with strangely weary limbs, locking herself alone into her room. Amusing! No book, indeed, was among the gold-topped bottles, or trinkets upon the dressing-table, or elsewhere around, except that on a table at her bed-head, where stood a small white ivory cross, lay one that would have opened in one's hands at many a page.   Drawing up a low chair, she leant her dark head against the pillow. "Thirty-two!" she said to herself, with a little, quivering smile—"thirty-two! Oh, why does one feel so young when one is growing old—yes, old! And yet, for one moment, I thought perhaps——. No matter.   I am rightly punished; and it is but natural Dick should care for the child.   Did she remind him of me, I wonder? . . . I was little older then!"

Back in thought she was forced to travel, and live over again the terrible conflict of her young life—the past soul-wrestlings; the agonies of a tender, doubting conscience. And so hard had been the battle, so uncertain the victory, that, even now—even now—she could not tell whether she had done wrongly, or wisely and well.

When her mother (a poor widow, of good family) had suddenly been left destitute, Miles Langton, as her only living relation, had been called upon to help in her affairs. Who knows? Perhaps even his petrified heart had warmed to her. Perhaps only, as unkind gossip averred, he had asked her to marry him, to save thereby the small allowance family pride forced him to give her. But she had married him—to gain a home for her daughter. Too soon she found his strange, shy nature suspiciously resented her love for her first husband's child ; and her failing life was troubled by fears lest she had sacrificed herself in vain, and the young daughter to whom her heart so fondly clung would have yet to battle alone with the rough world.

Just then Maud (in her fresh, girlish springtime) and a certain wild, generous scapegrace, had met each other for a few weeks—and loved! But their happy boy-and-girl courtship was brief, for, being in disgrace with the grand-uncle to whom he owed everything, the lad had been suddenly sent to Paris, through his grand-aunt's influence, who hoped he might sow his wild oats there, without reports of boyish pranks reaching her husband's vexed ears for some months.

Alas! stories of debts, wildness, gambling, and of his disinheritance by that uncle, soon reached the timid girl he had left behind. And she, herself made to feel so dependent upon Mr. Langton's alms that she had often begged leave to quit his roof, and go out as a governess, being only hindered by her mother's prayers, had, in youth's sudden despair, and passionate filial love—for that mother's sake, who said she *could* not end her weary death-sickness till her child was provided for—married old Mr. Lester, and thrown over Dick Newland!

Mother and daughter had both been cast in the same mould—sacrifice was so easy to each. But, in their great love for their dear

ones, high faith—in both timid, tender souls
—was forgotten in earthly, brooding care.
Ah! the youthful misery she remembered,
in the struggle between two opposing loves,
both of which were so great and strong.
Yet the one, as her fond, deluding spirit of
self-sacrifice whispered, was but a selfish
fancy—the other, the holiest God-implant-
ed instinct of her nature. And surely that
path must be the right one to tread which
caused her sharpest pain?

Women before have so reasoned, wel-
coming, in their humility and self-devotion,
any lot as good, that gave them alone the
pain and sorrow, sparing some they loved.
But the bitterness of the trial is only learnt
when they find too late—as Maud Lester
might—that their too great love has fallen
heavy upon others besides themselves, without the undue sacrifice availing those for
whom it was weakly offered up.

So Maud lived with her old husband.
Dick Newland came to be forgiven by

his grand-uncle. The fond, regretful mother passed this troubled, dim life's threshold. And people praised the rich young wife, though adding that her marriage was the one instance in which poor dear Mrs. Lester had shown herself terribly worldly—though they grew to add that she no doubt tried to atone for it by careful nursing for some years before her husband's death.

Those years had made the woman far stronger than the girl; tried by "man's true touchstone," she had ever ennobled. Often her loving heart but faulty judgment misled her, and worldly-wise folk smiled pityingly: often she stumbled and fell in her path, but as often she had risen again.

For near an hour her figure remained there, motionless, her soft, rather large hands, lying upon her lap, looking all the whiter against her mourning-black skirts. Then, dimly, a sweet, suffering face shadowed itself upon the memory, whereto she strove to recall it: the face of the mother over whose little child she had promised to watch, as that mother had watched over herself—even to devoted sacrifice—should any call for such occur in time.

And the time had come.

CHAPTER XVII.

"Only a woman's hair,
  A fair lock severed and dead ;
  But where is the maiden ?—where
  That delicate head ?

  Perhaps she is rich and fair,
  Perhaps she is poor and worn ;
  And 'twere better that one somewhere
  Had never been born."

Songs of Two Worlds.

"AND you never told me before that you knew Maud ? How strange of you, Colonel Cust !" exclaimed Miss Mab, reproachfully, to her tall companion, as soon as the gay party had started.

"How could I tell you ? I never even guessed you were the baby step-sister she used to speak of long ago. And you did not tell *me* Mrs. Lester was coming, or else——"

" Or else *what* ?"

" Or else I should sooner have congratulated her upon having a little sister who bids fair to rival her own charms," he lightly said, with a glance in his dark hazel eyes as he looked down at her, that implied, " a compliment, better or worse, ought to satisfy any woman's curiosity."

But the child stopped dead short, looking him full in the face; while her angry, luminous eyes took their fieriest colour.

" O! you very wise, clever—*stupid* man ! to think to yourself that that would flatter me !   As if I, or anyone, could ever be like Maud, when you might see with your own eyes there is no one fit to—to—" ("tie her shoe," was her vague thought; but reflecting that, as Maud's shoes were not tied, the expression might be old-fashioned, she loftily substituted)—"to stand in the same sunshine !"

" You seem very fond of her," was all he

said. " Is she so good to you, then ? "

As he had guessed, perhaps hoped, that question let loose the flow of her warm sisterly love and praise. Mabel used to declare that there were days when she could talk, and days upon which she could not (though the few friends she yet had privately considered the latter rare). This day, without doubt, was sacred to Vâk, the goddess of speech. All through the shuttered streets, crowded with parties of Sunday loiterers, and down into the low town, till they reached the field, her eager, gay chatter never ceased, except to wait for an assent to the eulogies, which yet, because Maud was her sister, the child, with a certain innocent tact, implied rather than expressed. Then, satisfied with his few quiet words or a fresh question, went on gaily again.

Behind them came Huntley, to whom Miss Mawkesworth, having marked him for her own, was faintly giggling about the very marked—ahem!—flirtation in front ! It was hardly necessary to call his attention to it. Poor Wat! Was he not even then comparing in thought handsome, rich, high-spirited Cust with his own poor, plain, sunburnt self? He said to his heart, with resignation, it was impossible now to doubt the evidence of his own senses, that the child had utterly changed to him since that fatal night—as certain that Cust had taken a strong hold upon her fancy. But, did he mean anything?

Watching his subdued, deferential manner, the musing air with which his eyes rested upon her, when she would utter something at which her own cheek glowed warmer as she spoke, Wat could not but fear he *did*. Yet, despite that great dread, he tried to tell himself he hoped so ! if the little one did indeed like him. " It would never do, though," was the end of his hardly cheerful thoughts. "He requires some one to give and take—or take without the giving." (He was thinking of Dick's well-known hot, passionate temper, and of the child's hitherto unbridled, if sweet, waywardness.)   "Fire and tinder!   If it gets as far as that, however, it will be no business of mine—none." And a slight sigh, fetched unwittingly from the depths of his honest, guileless heart, ended the matter.   To his surprise it was echoed.

.   "Were you ever (dear, dear; how forward you will think me, Captain Huntley!), but —were you ever *in love?*"

Wat sharply looked round; but then, surveying a moment her coy, averted head, softly replied, with what could only be called an unholy grin,

" I don't believe I could confide that to any other person, Miss Mawkesworth; but as *you* ask me—well, yes; once!   In—India."

" In India?"   She had expected to hear, " Harrogate;" and looking at Mab in front, prepared to hint, in gentle consolation, that other young ladies could be more appreciative than that forward little chit.   Now she repeated—"India!" in an impressive whisper, while her round eyes grew rounder. "Oh! how strange! I, too, know what it is to have suffered; but—won't you tell me *all* (as to a friend)? Indeed, in *me* you may confide utterly."

"Oh! if you like," quoth Wat, with surprising readiness, relieved to have diverted her attention. "We were quartered right up in the middle of India, you see, where hardly a married lady had ever been seen; and no girl within the memory of man. We were becoming savage and wicked, Miss Mawkesworth, and the best among us growing visibly thinner with pining after holier influences, when one blessed day came a strange report that a *young lady* would pass through! Such excitement! We held a monster meeting: decided to give her a ball. But, as somebody remembered she could not dance with everyone at once, it became a party; and—she accepted."

"La! how interesting!"

"She came! she conquered! You might have heard forty hearts beating in the silence as that young blushing angel entered. At last she consented to sing. We all closed round her, eyeing one another with jealousy, and wondering what the song might be as she softly began. Then out burst suddenly—

> 'They needn't come wooing to me,
> For my heart, my heart is over the sea!'

The man beside me actually dropped his eyeglass with vexation! He muttered,

"'Over the sea! over the sea! Then what *on earth* did she come here for?'"

Just then they saw those in front stopping to search on the ground for something. It was for a small old silver pencil-case of Mabel's, with which she knew her fingers had been idly playing at her watch-chain a few moments before. But after the whole party had helped her to look for some minutes in vain, she begged them not to stop their walk any longer on her account;

though Wat saw the child's face was vexed.

After about half an hour, they were returning, having seen all the different sulphur and iron wells which spring up wonderfully side by side. And only then Miss Mab took courage to put a question to Cust she had been some time revolving in her mind.

"Captain Huntley never followed us; did you see? Where can he be?"

"Oh! smoking somewhere at a stile," carelessly answered his friend, smiling. "I am afraid old Wat prefers his cigar even to such society as yours, my little lady."

Miss Higgins, who overheard both question and answer, looked at them both somewhat curiously.

A few yards farther they came upon Wat himself, who sauntered up to Mabel.

"Here is your pencil-case, Miss Langton. By good luck I happened to see it after you had gone."

She looked quickly up into his face; he was not smoking.

"Oh! I do believe you have been looking for it all this time—while we were amusing ourselves, too. I *do* thank you," she said, gratefully, under her breath.

"Don't mind," said Wat. "I thought you might be too much engaged, enjoying yourself, to talk to me much anyway; so I might just as well take a look for the pencil, when you seemed to value it."

"It is the only thing I can remember my mother giving me. The ring has grown thin, see, from constant wearing. But, Captain Huntley, I—might—have talked to you —a little."

She said it shyly and low, yet with a certain doubtful defiance, because so distrustful of her own treacherously weak heart already beginning to beat again; half wishful to show signs of friendship, yet still preserving her dignity as a fortress of retreat should Madame's evil predictions prove to contain the faintest shadow of truth.

"Would you? Well, I am glad to know

it, even now," he answered. Some slightest change in his tone made the little girl's heart throb still quicker; and, as once before at Brimham Rocks, she felt frightened of even talking without all the rest overhearing every word. Hastening her steps, she went on quickly—

"And there is one more thing—I ought to have thanked you before for the books. Really I am so very glad to have them; and I mean to wake up one hour earlier every morning, to study a little in peace."

Just then, in going through a gate, Cust joined her, and said in a low voice,

"Do tell me more about that rock-house you once built. Huntley is always happy, alone. He is not an ill-humoured animal like me. Besides, he would not care to hear about it—I do."

And though Wat would not try to hear the words, he caught the tone and a something of proprietorship in his handsome friend's manner—the friend he had himself asked the child to like.

Cust had no thought that he was selfish in this, for never a stray hint of gossip about the girl and Walter had reached his ears. He was only moody, and every moment more irritable; and she was to him like a happy pet canary that would trill and twitter for the asking, and so perhaps cheer him all the way back.

"You have charmed my evil spirit to rest this afternoon, as David did that of Solomon," was what he said to her as, on reaching the house, they separated.

But it is doubtful whether, an hour later, his valet would have corroborated the Colonel's statement, as he waited outside his master's door. It was perilously near the early dinner-hour; but twice already he had respectfully knocked, only to be rewarded by a deep, angry answer that though indistinct he could guess was a denial, well knowing the sound of danger.

" What a brute!" indignantly ejaculated after the third time a chambermaid, whom the susceptible Mr. Lawrence Delany had just waylaid to charm away the time.

" Ah! sure he has company. Don't be too hard upon him, Miss Mary Jane," blandly put in her fascinating adorer. " Neither of them likes to be interrupted."

" Why, who has he in there?" inquired Eve's vague curiosity.

" The divil! me dear," suavely whispered the polite Irishman, with a good foreign shrug as he pointed to the floor. " He's that fond, he comes bodily to visit the Colonel on occasions. At such times— since two's company but three is none, and having been brought up to bewtiful manners—I politely leave the gintlemen thegether."

Richard Cust was seated by his dressing-table, his head bent upon his hand; while from the lines on his face, and the additional swarthiness of his dark complexion, it would seem he had had far from pleasant thoughts. Beside him lay a tress of hair—a dark tress, with a wave in it, and a faint scent, as he fancied, still lingering around it. The handsome Colonel had many another curl in lockets, that had dangled in turns from his watch-chain; but this curl hardly ever saw the light. Those brown or golden locks only brought careless smiles to his lips; this called, with its every fine silken hair, aloud to all his memories of bitterness— the wild, vain regrets he had tried many a day and year to stifle! but which were now crowding upon him like evil demons; for that lock recalled what HAD BEEN.

"She supposed I would 'hardly remember her,'" he thought, with a smile of bitter self-derision. So calmly too—rather more calmly than when she wrote me that letter! I wish—I wish to Heaven I *had* forgotten her!"

Yet he had never been very bitter against Maud herself, except in the first rush of

youth's passionate despair and love, and in-
excusing anger; never been mean or unjust
enough to accuse her in heart one moment
of marrying for wealth. No! Her own
letter had clearly shown she had forced herself so to act, though with bitter pain, in ac-
cordance with her self-devotion, and with
what she believed to be right.

"They told her such slanderous gossip,
little wonder!" he thought to himself.
"Brought up, as she was, so pure, and only
too strict—knowing nothing of the world—
she was horror-stricken, of course; and, being
timid, was hasty."

Certainly he had been embarrassed that
time in Paris, but only in a slight degree
worse than had previously been the case.
Had she but waited! For in the end his
grand-uncle would have paid all; and Dick
himself would soon have overcome his grand-
aunt's wish for him to marry a neighbouring
heiress, which alone had prevented him

from telling her just then of his love for
Maud.

How different his life must have been,
had she been firm and married him! Without doubt he would have settled quietly
down; have reformed at once. No memories
should then have haunted him which had
better been flung deep into Lethe; no recol-
lections of wasted and reckless days and
nights, or "pallid dawns," staring in upon
him with their " dead men's eyes."

Yet he had now sufficient self-honesty to
own that had he taken her despairing fare-
well rightly instead of wrongly to heart, he
would not after it have gambled still more
wildly and deeply. He would not have gone
often and yet oftener to that old house in
the quiet Parisian street he so well remembered. Yes. He himself had allowed the
net to be drawn still closer around him by
that old Marquis de Warens (Marquis, for-
sooth! He ground his strong white teeth
at the recollection).

He would have been a free man now—
and Maud was free!

A half-sad smile of pleasure momentarily
lit the gloom of his face, as he fondly
imagined the WHAT MIGHT HAVE BEEN; but,
as he gazed vacantly in the glass, a dim reflection seemed as if to rise behind his shoulder—would take shape!

More clearly and more vividly memory
drew perforce the outlines of a young flaxen-
haired woman; fair, rather pretty, with an
oval face, drooping eyelids, and small but too
thin-lipped mouth; her almost colourless
hair drawn back over a cushion in French
fashion, with small lovelocks on either
temple.

Would no dim memory—no suggestion of
resemblance—stir within us also, could we
too see her with that quiet, demure air? Yet
none should she raise those frightened eyes;
vacuous, uninterested! it is the mere dull
gaze of wanting intellect.

She was dressed all in white, clasping a

bouquet of orange-flowers with both hands to her breast; and on that left hand was a new gold ring!

Dick Cust knew that phantomed shape only too well, for it signified to him WHAT WAS—and if he half-groaned in weary despair, drawing his hand across his eyes, little wonder! For that ring was the first link in a secret chain he had dragged for fourteen long years; and at times in his desperation he felt like one of those miserable slaves of old condemned, when their more happy comrade in the chains died, to remain manacled to the body of the dead.

END OF THE FIRST VOLUME.

PRINTED BY MACDONALD AND TUGWELL, BLENHEIM HOUSE.